MACW23
CHAPBOOK

ISBN: 9798864486955
Imprint: Independently published

The authors thank all
participants and facillitators in
the DCU MACW 2023 for their
creativity, counselling and
cheer.

DAN QUIGLEY

Dan Quigley is an amateur writer hailing from Wexford, Ireland. His day job is immersed in ophthalmic healthcare. However, after a decade spent as a "corporate sellout" (as dubbed by his mates) he decided to pursue his lifelong aspiration of becoming a professional writer, even if it meant aligning with the venerable Irish tradition of destitution, obscurity, and an indulgence in strong drink.

Dan has possessed a long-standing interest in the arts, but lacking the talent/ability/patience to pick up a musical instrument or a paintbrush, he instead opted for the "pen is mightier than the what-have-you" philosophy, and has been shoehorning clever-sounding phrases together on a laptop ever since, with mixed results.

Dan's writing lands upon a unique junction, merging

irreverent observations of contemporary Irish society, with speculative journeys into its mythological past. And sometimes, he likes to wax obnoxiously about those few months when he went abroad.

The accompanying story is one of the latter.

THE BEST SUNSET - DAN QUIGLEY

Through a gap in the canopy overhead, I watched the sun descend towards the treeline with a sinking feeling in my stomach, the full realisation of how screwed I was. Sweat ran down my face, and my clothes clung to me as if I had just clambered out of a bathtub. All around, the air thrummed with insects' wings and the everpresent shriek of cicadas. I was alone in the Cambodian jungle with the sun going down, completely and utterly lost.

This was all Marco's fault. I had got talking to the Italian backpacker over the clink of cutlery and tentative hum of conversation at breakfast that morning, in the familiarity of a seaside restaurant at the island resort where I was staying. Sitting at an adjacent table, all nonchalant poise in forest-sage Ray Bans and a salmon polo shirt, he leaned over to interject in my conversation with the waiter as I ordered my second coffee:

"Is the coffee good?"

"Best I've had so far. But don't get your hopes up," I replied.

He smiled in understanding; we were on a remote tropical island in a developing country. I had heard some constern rumours amongst fellow travellers of an airstrip being built further inland, always in tandem with much head-shaking as to how overdeveloped the area was becoming. But for now, most food and luxury items came to each individual business along the strip by sporadic boat drops, meaning both quality and quantity were hit or miss.

"A small price to pay for this, eh?" Marco nodded toward the white sand and turquoise waters just beyond the restaurant's bamboo railings, as though reading my thoughts. "Mind if I join you?"

I gestured an invitation. Making new acquaintances on the backpacker trails of Southeast Asia really was that simple. Marco pulled up a chair and introduced himself. He was a project manager for a software developer, based in Milan. He ordered avocado toast and a fruit salad. I surreptitiously pushed my own plate, empty but for the leftover grease of bacon and eggs, out of sight behind the condiment rack. We drank coffee and made small talk. It came easily when you were in a new place doing new things every few days. Where are you from? Where have you been so far? Where are you headed next? Typical 'backer bollocks,' to use the colourful Aussie phrase. The conversation turned to our reasons for being here.

"For me, the pressure of my job is just so-" Marco made an 'Up-to-here-in-shit' gesture, sawing the air by his neck, then wistfully shook his head, "So I'll take a few months to unwind, explore, then return refreshed. And you, Dan? What do you do?"

I took a sip of coffee to stall. That was a good question. I had quit my job as a lab technician to travel across the globe in search of *meaning*. Christ, what a dreadful cliché to admit to. I had acquired a TEFL qualification, and had some half-baked notion of teaching English in Vietnam, though I had yet to step foot in front of a class. I was no teacher. Was I a writer, then? The mere suggestion made me feel a charlatan; I hadn't written anything in months.

"I work in optics," I replied, brushing the question off, "Have you seen much of Koh Rong?"

"Just a little, these past few days!" he enthused, "There's a banana plantation in the hills, very insightful to see the locals at work up there. That way leads to Coconut Beach, up north. It feels much more natural than this strip, not so developed, you know...? But wait, have you been to the west side of the island?"

I hadn't.

"Ah! My friend," Marco clasped his hands together and waggled them emphatically. "You simply must go and see it! It's quite a walk, but there's a beach over there where you can watch the sunset right over the ocean." He turned his phone around to show me a picture of said spectacular sunset on his Instagram account, "A hidden gem! Off the beaten track. Not as touristy as this side, you know?"

And like an eejit, I believed the slick fucker. Standing in the jungle, I slapped a mosquito on my neck. Oh, I had waxed lyrical over such a grand idea. *That sounds great, Marco! an untouched beach; so much more authentic than this tourist trap!* Marco gave me directions to the start of a twisting trail that led through the jungle-covered hills, then advised me to catch a return boat that left the lone pier on the western beach, to ferry passengers back around to our side. *It leaves just after sunset, Dan, but be careful; that's the last one.*

If only that was my main concern now. Somewhere along the way, I had diverged off of that winding little path which Marco had shown me, onto an even smaller, more ephemeral byway, which locals must have traversed in search of suitable trees for firewood. It hadn't taken long to stray off that suggestion of a trail altogether, into the uniformly dense, forested hills. Off the beaten track; right.

I cast my gaze around the shadowy vined archways in a futile attempt to divine my next move. Unwillingly, my mind drifted back to a bar by the docks on the mainland, where backpackers got the ferry to Koh Rong from. I had stopped there for lunch two days ago while waiting for the next boat. There was an information graphic placed above the urinal in the men's room:

CAUTION:
There are 22 snake species
indigenous to Cambodia.
12 of these are venomous.
Please keep to main walkways.
Do not disturb leaf piles.

I stood motionless, eyeing piles of leaves in every direction. Of course I was wearing shorts, bare legs exposed to whatever fancied a bite. Of course there was no signal on my phone; remote island, developing country, far-removed from adequate medical facilities, in any case. Of course I hadn't told anyone where I was going that day, that would have been too sensible. Well, I conceded; Marco must know in an offhand way that I was planning to do this. Somehow I couldn't envisage him coming barrelling through the undergrowth to the rescue in his Moschino loafers.

After a few moment's dithering in that sodden furnace, my panic-induced paralysis was replaced by a comprehension that just standing here was the most surefire way to end up dead. No one was coming to help. And besides, I thought, a bold notion taking hold; how often had I daydreamed of testing my survival skills out in the wilderness, man against nature? Here was the chance! It was time to channel my inner Bear Grylls. Or better yet, that other survival guy on TV, who doesn't drink his own piss.

I realised that by following the direction of the setting sun, I must be heading west. It was an easy overhead marker to adhere to. The ground beneath me was an entirely different story. It was a ragged landscape of continuous dips and rises, covered in tangled bushes and vines that snared and scraped my plodding limbs. The soil was soft and liable to give way underfoot, adding an extra level of difficulty to traversing the constant slopes. The breathless humidity under the trees is almost impossible to describe, only to say that it felt far, far, more stifling than on the beach, where daytime temperatures regularly hit forty degrees Celsius.

And every square metre was alive with movement. Insects, crawling over every available surface and flying thick through saturated air; a multitude of exotic birds crying raucous, alien tattoos in the canopy above; and suspect rustling of larger animals hidden in the bushes. I even spotted a few small monkeys leaping from branch to branch in the murky distance. Mercifully, the only creatures to take a bite out of me had six legs, rather than none. They ate well that evening.

The gloom under the trees was growing profound when I finally burst into an open space. Above me, the sky had turned a lazy evening ochre. And in the distance lay the island's western sea, with the sun a radiant orb hovering over the waters of the Indian Ocean. I stepped forward with a surge of triumph reserved for the Edmund Hillarys and Tom Creans of the world, then stopped abruptly. About half a metre from where I stood, the ground dropped away in a sheer cliff. I edged forward and glanced down; a fifty foot drop at least. Superb.

No need to panic, What is it Bear Grylls always says? Improvise, Adapt, Overcome. Shy of drinking your own piss, it was solid advice. I reasoned that although lost, I couldn't have wandered too far from the trail intended to bring travellers east to west. There had to be a route down this cliff somewhere along here. So I followed the cliff edge left, towards the setting sun. It was easier going now out in the open, with a stirring of fresh air. The rock face eased into a marginally more shallow angle, and - There! A v-shaped crevasse in the cliff, and at its summit, hammered into a crack, was a metal rod with a red ribbon tied to it, fluttering in the whispers of a sea breeze that dared venture up to these heights. Approaching it, I followed the line of the crevasse downward to spot another rod maybe ten feet below, and another one further still. I was no rock climber, but my eyes could discern a navigable, albeit perilous route to the foot of the cliff. Well, you've come this far, Rambo. No turning back now.

The descent was a slow one, by necessity. The sun's rays were still intense as it shyly closed in to kiss the shimmering ocean, and the bare, day-baked rock under me radiated more heat, so that my pores redoubled their efforts to excrete every last drop of moisture from my body. Hard to say then, whether it was heatstroke or simply delirium from tiredness that had me mentally throttling Marco, while I should have been watching where I was planting my limbs. One small, stomach-dropping slip brought my attention sharply back to the present, as my hands scrabbled to find purchase and pebbles skittered down the slope.

Finally and with no small relief, I stepped onto flat land again. The area was elevated above more trees which led gently down to the ocean. From here, I could actually see the sands of the fabled western beach beyond the green expanse. It wasn't that far. But I wouldn't make it down in time for the sunset. Strangely, that realisation didn't bother me. After the unprecedented ordeal which I had just endured, it felt more fitting, somehow, to view it up here on the heights, alone. That golden orb which I had followed as a saviour all day, and which had followed me in return, composed a chromatic masterpiece of crimson and magenta as it silently departed beyond the horizon line. Just a few quiet, solitary minutes. Then it was gone. After all that. Marco had been right about one thing, at least. That sunset was magnificent.

So engrossed was I in the spectacle that I hadn't realised

what I was standing on, a wide swathe of red-raw levelled earth, stripped of foliage by mechanical means. The torn tree stumps around its edges told the story. And there, in the distance behind me, was the bright yellow outline of a bulldozer. The dimensions of this scar in the landscape suddenly clicked. So. The rumours of an airstrip were true.

I felt a strange internal conflict at this discovery; the disgust of bearing witness to the churned earth and destroyed habitat, juxtaposed with a growing sense that my presence on the island, blundering western buffoon that I was, was contributing to the necessity of such an airstrip in the first place. Not unlike the frustration of sitting in a traffic jam; you're not just experiencing it, you are it.

The faint sound of waves lapping the shore tugged me from my introspection. It was time to move again. The jungle between the airstrip and beach descended in an easy decline of sparser trees than the hills above, and it wasn't long before I found myself trudging through white sand, making a beeline for the ocean. I collapsed headlong into the shallows, into a euphoria of blessed coolness, while simultaneously, the saltwater lit up a constellation of cuts, scrapes, and insect bites which I had amassed all over my body during the trek. I pressed into further depths and twisted around, to float serenely on my back for a few minutes, before a thought occurred to me. Curious, I stood upright and looked back at the beach. Completely deserted. Strange. Marco did say it was quiet here, but surely -

The sudden blast of a horn turned my head. I squinted at a distant concrete pier. A singular boat belched smoke from its chimney as engines and a PA system roared into life. I could discern a mass of bodies onboard moving through disco lights on a canopied deck. Even from this distance, the music sounded tacky and abrasive.

I shook my head at such a contrived party atmosphere. Tourists. The sight of it jarred my sensibilities after the solemn sunset, along with the gut-punch of forest destruction in the hills above. Then came the realisation that the offensively loud boat labouring into the open water was, in fact, the last boat back to the west side of the island, which Marco had warned me about.

Fuck. Okay, remain calm. I am Rambo. I am that guy that isn't Bear Grylls. There will be no piss imbibed today. I waded back to shore and began ambling up the beach towards the pier in as unpanicked a fashion as I could manifest.

Perusal of a laminated sign attached to a wooden post confirmed my worst fears. So, was it to be another hike back through the jungle hills, now in the dark? My body balked at the idea; it simply wasn't an option. I cast my eyes around. At the corner of the beach in the rapidly gathering dusk, I noticed the moving outlines of a Khmer couple packing up a freezer box with unsold beer and soft drink cans.

"Suostei," A man about my own age cheerfully greeted the sweaty, bedraggled, Westerner rambling towards him. "You need a ride, bro?"

Evidently, lost gobshites like myself weren't such an anomaly. The Khmer on the islands were mostly city folk who moved down for the tourist season, loath to miss a business opportunity.

"How much?"

"Twenty dollars?" He ventured. It was an outrageous price, probably several days wages for him. I'd have paid it in a heartbeat.

"I've got ten on me, man."

A brief discussion between the man and his woman. He shrugged.

"Okay, very good," He gestured back towards the treeline,

"Let's go find my brother."

He led me away from the beach a short distance into the jungle, to a clearing where more men lay resting with feet raised in hammocks. The light of a blaring TV cast ghostly white luminance and long shadows through the trees. To this day, I haven't figured out how they powered it.

The man cupped his hands and called into the clearing. Momentarily, there came a gruff response. A figure dismounted from his hammock and approached us. Another curt exchange in Khmer, as the first man pointed me out and relayed the situation. The shifting light of the TV fell across the brother, and I saw that he couldn't have been a day over fifteen. The kid looked me up and down with ill-concealed contempt. But it seemed he had been offered a lucrative split of the takings. He beckoned me to follow him.

"His bike has a headlight," the first man declared, presumably in an attempt to be reassuring, since it was fully dark by this point. I was not reassured. But the whole situation had by this point become so farfetched, so comically out of my control, that my ability to assess risk had long since been abandoned somewhere in the murk of the jungle. I clambered onto the seat behind the Khmer kid, feeling the thrum of the engine reverberate through my crotch and down my legs. I didn't bother asking for a helmet; they were a rarity in the mainland cities, unheard of out here.

My hitherto sojourns through Southeast Asia had made me as comfortable with hopping on the back of a motorcycle with a stranger as one can be. Nonetheless, I was painfully aware of my wet t-shirt from diving in the ocean just fifteen minutes previously, not to mention how abysmal my body odour must have been after that trek, as I leaned forward to press into his back and gripped the handholds either side of the seat.

As if in retribution, the kid kicked us forward away from the clearing without ceremony, accelerating furiously down the dirt road. My last fleeting sight of my saviour, the big brother, was his expression turning from an encouraging 'wave-for-the-tourist' smile, to a clear 'OH-SHIT' as the bike roared past him into the night.

We hurtled along the dirt road at breakneck speed, wind whipping past us as the trees and foliage blurred into a featureless streak of black and green. Every bump and dip sent a jolt through my body, and both of the bike's wheels went fully airborne on numerous occasions. I shouldn't have been surprised; children here rode bikes as soon as their legs were long enough to reach the ground. But even so, I had a suspicion that this kid was showing off. Because I was taller than my driver, I had the misfortune of being able to see over his shoulder. The narrow triangle illuminated by his headlight didn't reveal much, but as we slalomed further along the track, I could ascertain that to our right side was another cliff, this one dropping into the sea. My chauffeur did not seem nearly as averse to this fact as I was, as he bobbed and weaved across the pitted surface.

After an interminable length of time, the lights of my resort began to twinkle in the distance. As we approached the more populous area, it became apparent that the kid only had a vague idea of how to get to the main strip. We detoured firstly through the back gardens of some luxury chalets, splattering mud over their immaculate white walls with spinning tyres, then through a large clearing which was being used as a semi-permanent concert site for tourists, where a group of enterprising Westerners were setting up for the night. I had a mere second to spy an encased bundle of cables running from a generator to the stage laying across the open ground in front of us, before there was an emphatic crunch and I was jolted in my seat. I didn't dare look back, but even over the bike's roar I heard an incredulous French accent;

"Are you fucking kidding me?!"

At last, the bike slowed to a stop on the main strip. I dismounted, clumsy as a newborn foal, and turned to face the kid. He was already revving his engine, eager to be gone.

"Thank you," I croaked. I slapped ten dollars into his palm, trying to appear nonchalant; not as if my testicles had taken up residence in my ribcage. He just nodded, the merest suggestion of a smile curling the corners of his mouth, before disappearing into the dark, leaving me to wobble up a side street towards my accommodation.

My room was essentially a space in a corrugated iron shed filled with MDF partitions which didn't reach the ceiling. It created faux rooms, where you could hear your neighbours talking, arguing or having sex clearly as if you were standing next to them. Birds inhabited the rafters overhead, and cried out at odd hours. It felt deafeningly quiet as I staggered in, closed the door behind me and slowly sank to the floor.

My heart still thundered in my chest, and my mind wandered, drunk with giddy exhaustion. I gazed upward, past the whirring overhead fan to the single bare lightbulb. The gravity of the day's events began to press down with that draft of air, and the aches and pains beginning to make themselves known throughout my body. It was the strangest contradiction of exhaustion and exhilaration I ever felt.

The naked light burned an image into my eyes; not of a lone bulb, but of a crimson sunset, hanging over a glistening sea in eternity. An ocean who's name seemed so full of exotic promise, and yet, was not altogether unlike the sea I had lain eyes over almost every day as a child. That sun on Koh Rong overlooked an entire world which I could only move through fleetingly, as a stranger. But that brief, fraught experience had left an indelible lesson, which no Instagram picture could ever articulate.

RALPH MILLS

Ralph graduated from Durham University in 1992 with a degree in English Literature. He taught English in Barcelona, then for the next two decades he wrote and edited web content for a number of organisations in London, Chicago and Dublin.

He coaches junior athletics and rugby, and founded the women's rugby programme at Clontarf RFC. He still turns out on occasion for Clontarf *Golden Oldies*. He is also a licensed practitioner of traditional Chinese acupuncture.

He has written two novels – the sci-fi epic *Steampunk Odysseus* and the historical fantasy romance The Storm's Daughter. He lives in Clontarf with his wife and two children.

MUM'S FINAL SAY - RALPH MILLS

The last time I saw her
she was plugged in to a machine
that quietly hissed.
She was tiny and brittle, yet fiercely, still,
she stared down death
over the parapet of her bed-chart.
I mawked some parting words
to fill the wheezing quiet
and thank her for her life, and mine,
and tamp some resolution into her awaiting grave
so that softly she might lie.
For half an hour I rambled on
'til she reached for the nearest magazine -
a 'Hello' with the Duchess on the front -
and she said '*I'll let you go now.*'
Eventually I got the hint
and let her go.

UNDIAGNOSED - RALPH MILLS

Following my father's death, I was packing up our family home of forty-five years. Dad had been allowed to accumulate a lot of clutter in the loft because my mum was far too small to reach the pull-cord on the hatch. She never suspected that every time she made him clear his piles of bric-a-brac from the utility room, that was where it went. I found abstracts from his four decades in pharmaceutical research, abortive wood-whittling projects, a scale model of our house he had made for my sister's dolls, and boxes of components for classic cars he never got to own.

And then, amongst the detritus of a life crammed with eclectic passions, I found an old leather suitcase. It was full of letters, written in his distinctive hand, which I had perfected as a schoolboy in order to sign my own terrible report cards. They were all addressed to Mum.

He had met her in his mid-twenties when he returned from his post-Doctorate in North Carolina. Dad was an acolyte of The Goon Show and a lover of jazz; a goofy giant from the terraces of North Manchester whose mother had funded his education by scrubbing steps in the well-to-do neighbourhoods. Mum was one of five daughters of a patrician headmaster from the grand suburbs of Preston.

They met at a dance. Mum was sitting on one man's knee while another lit her cigarette. Dad thought he didn't have a chance. But she liked men who made her laugh, and Dad was an extremely, surreally funny man. He was six-foot-four tall; she was four-foot-ten. She was hyperactive and prone to stress; he was horizontally relaxed. Each was everything the other wasn't.

The letters spoke in cheerful prose of a life I never knew

they'd had. He had taken a job in Lancashire, while she was still down in Hertfordshire, and for the six months they were apart he would write every week on company stationery. His was a tender infatuation, unencumbered by the responsibilities of parenthood. He was continually falling off his motorbike while visiting her in atrocious weather. They ate baked beans for a month to save for the deposit on their first bungalow so they could be together. Though he was always warm and had a sparkling imagination, I had thought of him more as a man of science than of romance. Yet each letter was signed off with the same dedication, the raw adoration of which caught me in my throat. "I will love you forever," it said.

In the three years following Mum's death, Dad suffered from heart failure. None of his doctors saw any relevance in the fact that he had just lost his beloved wife of fifty years - there was nothing in the ECG scans to indicate the fact. But if they were looking for an overriding cause of death to put on the certificate, I might have suggested 'Takotsubo's Cardiomyopathy.' That's the clinical term for a broken heart.

II BEREAVEMENT - RALPH MILLS

The tent is being dismantled
The stars are lying down
The aftershow is cancelled
The circus has left town

The playthings are back in their box
The playmates all have left
The hands hold still on carriage clocks
The curtains hang bereft

The teachers finally know the truth
The cause of death is inked
The hearse has passed the watchman's booth
And childhood is extinct

The priest has delivered his platitudes
As set down in his book
I've shaken hands with gratitude
At the trouble everyone took

Aunties have left their cups of tea
and talk of happier days
Voices that waft past parlour doors
Have receded into haze

I search the house for a familiar face
Of one who has always been
But those who brought me to this place
are nowhere to be seen

KIERAN MARSH

I have been writing for many years with varying degrees of success, but still I'm delighted at what I have learned about myself and my writing from the course. I feel I'm on a trajectory if not to publication, then at least to being able to enjoy my writing and know that I am crafting as well as I am capable.

For this selection I have chosen an old story which has been one of my most successful shorts, being featured in Ciaran Carty's New Irish Writing in 2013. I'm also throwing in a couple of poems; I haven't written poetry in twenty years and I've been astonished at how much I've enjoyed it again.

You can find more of my work on *gooseberryseason.com*

THICKENED WITH BLOOD - KIERAN MARSH

The stains of death still mark me. I mean, I'm only fifteen, I'm supposed to be, you know, flirting with boys, not floating about like Casper the Friendly Ghost.

Mom is still mourning. She thinks that she's at last put it behind her, that her passion for cooking has saved her. She's going to compete, you see. Masterchef. A long time ago, that other lifetime, she wrote off to apply. Dabbled away at custards and petits fours. Then, just after... Well, after I died, the date came through. She panicked and gave up completely, then started fervently cooking, and she's been flopping between extremes since then.

'Oh, to hell with it. I shouldn't be doing this, Isabel. What kind of bloody fool...'

She talks to me all the time. I like that, even though she can't see me and I can't talk back. I like it even though she can be such a whinger.

'My sweet, my little Isabel, this is just stupid. Why do I not just stop?'

Hey ho, I can say nothing to help, that's what you get when you're dead. I stroke her forehead, but she feels nothing, not even the tiny breeze that ruffles the loose hair hanging down over her face. She is befloured, like she is about to deep fry herself.

'Forecmeat? Am I mad? Yes, yes, totally fruit loops. But that's why you love me, right?'

So she's done all her techniques, like, you know, the sauces Hollandaise and Bernaise, gutting fishes and boning chickens; now she is focussing on some signature dishes. I mean, signature dishes? Like she's a proper chef? Okay, she is a proper chef and I love her and I should be encouraging and all. Except that I can't be discouraging not matter how I try, since I'm dead. Did I mention that?

It's become too much, I think. What do they call it? Obsessive compulsive or something? Mom listens to Radio 4 a lot, Women's Hour and all that, and they talked about people trapped in cycles of behaviour. She nodded wisely as she listened but couldn't see herself in it. Seven hours she's been in the kitchen today; pies, tarts, a delicate consommé have all been produced. Who is going to eat it all? Dad and Pete and Barry just want burgers and chips, for God's sake. It has consumed her, or consomméed her perhaps, and I worry. I'm only fifteen and I shouldn't worry, but I bear the stains of death.

The door bursts open, almost explodes, and a bundle of boys rolls in. What's the collective noun for boys? A mess?

'Hiya,' says Dad, grinning.

'Mud!' Mom points her finger-of-power at the three of them, then at the floor she's washed twice already today.

Dad shambles forward, trailing dirt. 'Give us a hug.' He approaches with arms spread, she pushes him off but he enfolds her in a sweaty embrace. She thumps at his back, playfully, and he lifts her, ook-ing like a chimpanzee. Barry, who is twelve, turns his head in disgust and slouches out the door.

'Upstairs, the lot of you, shower, now.' Mom is serious again.

Pete looks up at me, with his inside eyes.

'Hiya, sis,' he says. Pete is only five, so he knows I am there and we can chat, which is brilliant, but it is sad too because he is already growing too old. Sometimes he does not see me for days.

'Hi, Petey. Do anything good?'

'We kicked ball, and Dad fell in the mud and said don't tell Mom.'

'Better not tell Mom then.'

I laugh, he laughs, and for a moment I feel what life is like, but that isn't for me, not my gift any more. Hey ho!

'Is Dad doing okay?'

'Oh, you know. He's sad sometimes, but he pretends not to.'

'He's trying to protect you, I guess.'

'Grown ups are silly.'

'Oh, Petey, you don't know how silly.'

The meat makes a smacking sound as Mom drops it on the cutting board, like a cadaver on a slab. Three hares, naked, skinless. No pelts, no heads, no claws - brutal, real, visceral. I look at Mom as she inspects them. There's horror in her face. She saw them already, of course. She bought them from a man she met at a farmers market. He owns a farm in Wiltshire with good hunting on it, apparently; trying to source direct from the supplier, you see, very posh and Masterchef-y. So he insisted on bringing them to the house, very interested in helping her, he said. Brought in half a dozen and made the poor woman pick out the best three, giving his advice on the leanness and age of the beasts. She could barely hold herself together while she pointed.

Today, she loses it completely and she's bawling. There's snot and tears as she lets it out. I hug her; I try to hug her. I cannot feel her or she me, but I just need to believe I'm reaching out to her.

'Oh, look at these things, Isabel, these lifeless... bloody...'

The ugliness and brutality of the dead beasts is overwhelming for her, while for me, it's part of the cycle, the game we all play, life, death. Such stark words from one so young, but that's how things are when you're dead.

I feel the creatures fading memory, its mark on mind. It sits in a glade, a broad swathe of bushes and straggling trees surrounded by wintry scrub grass. I feel its vitality as it sniffs at the air, nose twitching. Something alien is coming. The hare stiffens.

Immeasurable moments pass. Still, be still. Something comes in sight, sniffing the undergrowth, a dog. The hare bolts.

I feel the glory of its pace, all that is exalted and beatific in nature is captured in its gait. Forelegs stretch earnestly, hind legs drive with pure energy. The dog is chasing, but it is slow and clumsy by comparison.

The hare is nearly away. Something kicks it. Something unseen hits it with all the force of creation, throwing it head over heels, leaving it lying prone, paralysed. A moment later, a horrific bang.

The teeth of the dog close about it, but it is still alive. Its slack body is carried to another creature. A man. A hunter. The man lifts the hare by the back legs. He takes the neck and... Takes the neck and...

...And I'm dead again.

The cooking continues, but Mom's still sobbing quietly. The book is open. Mrs Beeton, for goodness' sake. No level of pretension is beneath her dignity when Masterchef comes calling.

I jest, but I'm not at all happy. There's a shadow hovering about her, a stain, and I look at the stain that marks me. It's growing on her, too. I don't understand, but she loses hope every day, and as she does, that stain deepens.

'Oh, this is no good. Bloody... bones...'

She's struggling with her chef's knife to quarter the carcass, reading Mrs Beeton's advice about where to insert her blade in order to cleanly cleave the breast bone.

Dad and Pete come bounding down the stairs, all clean and shiny. They come in to see how she's getting on.

'Ah, come on,' Dad says. 'Let me see a smile.'

'Just lay off.'

'Let's be having you.' He goes to grab her and squeeze her, but he's misjudged her mood; she twists out of his grip, bloody knife flashing.

'No! Get off me.'

'Get up with you now,' Dad laughs, pulling at her skirt.

'Stop!' Mom shouts. 'I'm just... I'm...'

'You're taking it too seriously, is what you are.'

'Too seriously? Too bloody seriously?' She thumps him. There's no playfulness in it this time.

'Now stop that...' He points a finger as if she's a misbehaving child, she slaps at him again. For a moment the knife is waved, then she drops it and turns, crying.

Pete runs. He goes up to his room, and I follow. He hates it when Mom and Dad snap at each other. I find him on his bed, with his favourite book, The Velveteen Rabbit. He holds it open and I read to him.

I look at the illustrations, the Rabbit with his sad, saggy velveteen skin, and my mind twists back to the echo-memory that is buried in the hare carcass downstairs. Neck freshly broken, the hunter takes his knife to it, ripping skin from flesh. He slices open its belly and, twisting it backwards, flicks the guts out into a tub, making a wet slurp. Blood, pouring from the broken diaphragm, sprays into tub, a rich hot stream. Blood, flesh, bone and sinew, rough ingredients of life now reduced to ingredients.

I imagine how it would be for my tears to flow onto the pages of the Velveteen Rabbit, but I cannot cry, I'm dry as dust.

Pete joins Dad and Barry watching the footie on the telly. Peace settles. Liverpool draw with Everton, Man U kick off, Mom watches moment by moment as the meat softens into the stew, seasoning with her heart and soul. At last, she's at the final step.

'Add hare's blood to taste,' she reads. 'To taste? What the hell's that supposed to mean?'

She sighs, shoulders slump, like she's ready to dump the whole pot. Then something changes on her face, a candle lighting.

'Be with me, Isabel. Hold my hand. Be by my side, won't you? I know I can do this, but I need you.'

'I'm here, Mom,' I say, soundless. I hold her hand, fleshless. I stay with her, absent, and yet...

She takes a tupperware out of the fridge. The man brought that too, the blood freshly cut from the hares. She pours it, dark red stain, reflecting the work of the hunter, remembering the moment of life leaving, like...

Like that day on the beach. Pete and I dug sand castles, we made sand soup, and Mom and Dad laughed. They were tired, I'd been in hospital for a week.

Then it came on me, the bleeding. Mom tried to staunch it with a towel, but it was too strong, too fast, too much. That stain, that flow.

Mom watches it. She doesn't cry. The sauce boils and the blood thickens; like my blood never would. After several minutes, she tastes it and nods.

'It is done.' Christ on his cross, yielding His soul to the Lord. 'It is done.'

Dad comes in to help her plate up, pieces of hare delicately balanced on creamy mash, forcemeat balls arranged in the reduced jus.

'Wow,' he says, 'that smells fabulous. I mean, that's it,

restaurant standard. You're gonna knock them backwards.'

She kisses him, he carries two plates to the dining room.

I'm dead. And, some day, she will die too, but not yet. Not yet. Hey ho.

She takes up two plates and, just before she flicks off the light with her elbow, she blows a kiss to me.

'Good night, beautiful.'

TREE WALK IN ST ANNE'S PARK - KIERAN MARSH

Path ploughed with mud,
Plush plosh slisch shloosch.
Ornamental boulevard,
An arborland of time-twisted trees
That brings us by a commodius vicus
Past a vacancy that was the Guinness palace.
Here once the Lords and Ladies Ardilaun
Enjoyed privilege that is now everybody's prerogative.
Shloosch plompf klimp cnumph,

And here three years past I passed this place
And I remember well as I walk,
Like an aroma remembers the occasion,
That I was coated in anxiety,
Layer upon layer
So that even as the cnumph flunch grosh gloosh
Ran slime up the side of my boot
So the toxic slime of worry,
    Of work,
        Of woe,
            Of horror,
                Of hell on earth while sitting at my desk
Washed over and over me in waves.
No birdsong could exorcise it.
No sea breeze could blow it
From out of the dark corners of my head.
These trees remember.
They bent then to my attention,
Caring boughs offered balms
Reaching to my pain.
But the care has to start inside.
The care has to start inside.
Plush plosh slisch shloosch.
And now with a glorious smile
    I slough off my shoes
        And bathe my toes
            In the warm mud
                Of my hard won wellbeing.

THE FOX AND THE HOUND

Midnight, the hound must head out,
Walking must be done, the rule of dogs.
Silent. Night silent. Sleep silent.
Yet the hum of city never sleeping.
Hwæt. The hound goes hard,
Strains on leash, stares at length,
The sound from its mouth a whimper of hunger,
Nature is never far from the surface.

Then there she is, the fox, the sionnach,
Creature of cunning, bold red coat,
Brilliant eyes brighten the gloom
As gladly I stare on her
And she stares back
Knowing the hound is held,
Gleaming, goading, glaring.
Then she's off, checking the road for cars,
Off to grub in gardens,
Find food for fox cubs,
Make music in the summer evening.
She has a freedom beyond us all.

And the hound, all nature quelled,
Crawls home to kibble
And quilts and couches
And comfort and cleanliness.
And she will lie and dream of the fox
And dream of its fleet feet
And its noble glare
And know that she is tame.

DIMITRIS POLITIS

Dimitris Politis was born in Athens Greece. He studied Economics in Piraeus University in Greece, followed by a BA in Classics and Italian language and literature in University College Dublin, followed by an MA in European studies and Communications at Trinity College Dublin, from where he graduated in 1994. Dimitris has lived in Greece, Ireland, UK, Belgium and Luxembourg, while working for several EU Institutions. He has published several specialised articles and reviews related to working conditions and health and safety at work in English, French, Greek and Italian. His first novel "The stolen life of a cheerful man" was published in Greek in Athens in October 2012. His second novel "The next stop" was published in Greek in October 2019. Several of his Greek short stories have been published in literary magazines and websites after winning awards and distinctions in online and live events. Several of his short stories in English have also been published in three Anthologies. He has been a leading member of the English speaking "Brussels Writers Circle" since 2012. He currently shares his life between Brussels and Sallins, Co. Kildare, finishing an MA in Creative Writing with Dublin City University.

AN ORDINARY BRUSSELS DAY - DIMITRIS POLITIS

Another Brussels Day, I gently stoked my beard, examining my scruffy morning reflection in the bathroom mirror. *14 years here today...* I felt the delicate perfume of the shaving foam, while my warm razor blade decapitated every single hair like a minuscule guillotine, followed by the shower gel fragrance as each drop's abrasive freshness attacked my body.

In the kitchen, the steaming dark juice dripping through the rumbling coffee machine permeated my nostrils with its intoxicating aroma. I filled a cup, my eyes fixated on the hands of the clock across the counter.

Minutes later, I followed my habitual steps to the metro. The Brussels sky had already started to light up. Its pale blue, timid attempt to mock the colourless apathy of the city, was gradually getting stronger.

The oversweet smell from the Metro Waffles stand assaulted me, as my office preoccupations were attacking my brain: priorities, deadlines, administrative procedures...

The tin-coloured metro carriage dragged itself hissing in front of my feet and I breezed in with a quick leap. The lingering waffles scent was replaced by the odour of the huddle, of accumulated morning breaths, of thick, stale air. At the next stop, a pretty woman in her forties came in and stood across from me. Her bright red coat stood out among the gloomy winter clothing of our travelling companions. Absorbed in the screen of her mobile phone, she remained totally oblivious to the crimson aura she spread around her.

Seven stops later, my station was announced: «Maalbeek». I was among the first to jump out through the carriage sliding doors, heading with brisk steps to the nearest escalator. A loud, garbled howl made me stop and turn my head back. An intense, blinding blaze attacked my eyes with a thousand colours, a myriad of molecules from colourful fragmented glass. Assailed by a deafening, rumbling sound, by flaring flames, by a silver rain of murderous nails, by a golden burning sensation, I was violently thrown down to the ground, my face pressed against the grimy floor tiles.

Darkness.

Deadly silence.

I tried hard to open my eyes. White dust, flying everywhere, made them sting and crinkle. A cacophony of random screams and noises accompanied by a frantic mobility conquered the disastrous disorder of the scene. Milky shadows, ghosts in the white fog of dust, ran right and left in panic, like rats caught in a trap. Incomprehensible voices, incomprehensible languages, wild cries and screaming, a desperate baby shrieking, lost in the battered scene.

Time passed.

I opened my eyes again. No tingle. The atmosphere was now clean, almost dusted. A light breeze caressed my face. Lying on a stretcher, I was gazing at the morning sky: a soft, pale blue was announcing the arrival of spring.

I turned my head as I felt a gentle squeeze on my left arm. An ebony-skinned woman, dressed in white looked straight to my eyes: "My name is Amina, try not to move. We will put you in the ambulance shortly. You will be OK." The corner of my left eye caught the person laying on the stretcher next to me: my elegant travelling companion in red appeared to be conscious, communicating with her stretcher carrier: *She is alive!*

Hours later, in my hospital bed, abandoned for a brief moment by my medical saviours and my preoccupied visitors, I strove to make sense of what had just happened, to identify if I felt more relieved, angry, confused, desperate or numb. *Not an ordinary Brussels Day after all...* I felt the warmth of the last sunset rays invading my 10th floor hospital room, elated for having escaped the morbid list of the 32 souls consumed by the terrorists' nail bombs that morning.

* * * * * * *

The above piece is dedicated to all people who have lived through and survived the trauma of a terrorist attack and especially to Shanti De Corte, who despite surviving unscathed the Brussels terrorist bombings of March 2016, decided in 2022 to be legally euthanised rather than continue to live with the trauma of these events. Shanti was a 17-year-old student travelling with her classmates from Brussels Airport when the terrorists detonated their bomb in the crowded departures area. Although not physically injured in the attack, she endured years of panic attacks and depression afterwards. She tried twice to take own life in 2018 and 2020 and posted regularly on social media about her struggles. "With all the medication I take, I feel like a ghost. I can feel nothing anymore... My soul is empty. Maybe there are other solutions than medication..." she wrote in 2019. Shanti finally chose to be euthanised on 7 May 2022 at the age of 23, with the full support of her family, after two independent psychiatrists approved her official request. Antwerp prosecutors later began an investigation into her case after Paul Deltenre, a neurologist at the Brugmann University Hospital in Brussels, complained that the young woman's decision to end her life "was made prematurely." The case was officially closed in October 2022 after the Court found that "no errors or violations were committed in the euthanasia procedure". Euthanasia has been legal in Belgium since 2002 and people suffering from illnesses deemed incurable or unbearable have the right to ask a physician to administer a fatal dose, even if the ailment is psychiatric.

The March 2016 blasts at Brussels airport and Brussels Maalbeek metro station killed 33 people including Shanti and left more than 340 injured. The high-profile trial of those accused of being responsible started in Brussels on 12 September 2022 and is still ongoing.
Dimitris Politis, March 2023.

SUSAN CONDON

Susan Condon is currently an MA in Creative Writing student at Dublin City University and has previously studied writing in NUI Maynooth and the Irish Writers Centre.

Susan's short stories and poems have won many awards, including first prize in the Jonathan Swift Award and SDCC Short Story and Poetry competitions. Stories have also been Long Listed, on four occasions, in the RTÉ Guide/Penguin Ireland Competitions and aired on The Jealous Wall and StoryMap.

Writing has been internationally published, including: Boyne Berries, Flash Fiction Magazine (USA), Flash Flood Journal, Live Encounters (Indonesia), My Weekly (UK) and Spelk and anthologised in a number of outlets, such as, Ireland's Own, Circle & Square and The Lea-Green Down.

Susan blogs at: www.susancondon.wordpress.com and Tweets @SusanCondon

PHOTOGRAPH OF A STRANGER - SUSAN CONDON

My eyes grow tired, as they focus on the black and white images of ghosts from my past.

The thin, rectangle stuck to the wall bears no resemblance to the bulky, square box I remember, taking pride-of-place in the front room. Two knobs protruded; one to turn the set on; the other to switch from one channel to the other. A set of rabbit's ears perched patiently on top; like a halved orange, placed flat side down and pierced with a pair of steel knitting needles. My older brother Joe, convinced us that Martians were tracking us through them, whenever we tuned in the TV.

Joe is long-dead, but not before he headed to the United States of America and made his fortune. He sent home money to support the rest of the family, during those lean years, and every Christmas a box would arrive full of wonderful presents. It was usually beautiful, coloured silk scarves for my mother and three older sisters and a new hat for father, but he would always send something exciting for Jimmy and me. The most memorable present, was a set of gliders, made from coloured paper with a brass tip at the nose. Jimmy was the oldest, so he had first choice. He chose the blue glider, so I had the red one. Every child at school wanted to be our friend that winter, as we tested out our aeronautical skills against each other. The airplanes would swoop and glide through the air as we ran along whooping with delight.

I lift my head and look out into the garden. The sky is blue, the sun fighting to appear and there is a hint of a rainbow. It would have been the perfect day to fly. I feel my forefinger and thumb twitch, itching to hold the glider between them, bending the wings just the right degree to ensure that mine would fly the farthest. I look down at the gnarled hands in my lap as I wonder where my life has disappeared to.

I hear soft-soled footsteps and a man appears with a tray. He places it on the table in front of me. It smells good.

"Here you are Dan, chicken soup, your favourite."

He places a napkin into my shirt collar and spoons soup into my mouth. It tastes as good as it looks, warm and creamy with a little white pepper.

"I'll do it myself," I say. He does not seem to hear me. No-one ever seems to. I try to take the spoon from him, but my hand shakes and he pushes it down, gently but firmly.

"Let me help you, Dan. Would you like some bread, you can dip it into the end of the bowl?"

I nod and hold a piece of dry bread, ready to mop up every last drop.

"It's Wednesday today Dan, Grace will be in to visit you later. We better get you spruced up and looking nice for her."

I nod my head. I don't know who Grace is; but it will be nice to have a visitor. He combs my hair, tugging it to the side and holds up a small mirror. An old, grey-haired man with blue eyes smiles back at me. As I move closer to the mirror, he does too, and I can see that he is in need of a shave. It is just a light stubble but I always prefer a close shave myself. I rub a hand across my chin. The man in the soft-soled shoes laughs.

"I'm not a fan of those electric shavers either, Dan," he looks at his watch, "we've just enough time to give you a proper shave before she comes." He places a hand on my shoulder, "I'll be back, in just a minute." He picks up the tray and I can hear his light footsteps as they fade down the hall.

The rainbow has become hazier and there is a light rain on the window pane, maybe not the best day for paper gliders, after all. It reminds me of the day my glider caught in Mrs Kennedy's tree. As I climbed higher and higher into the leaves, she came out her front door, stood below, with her arms folded and threatened to tell mother.

But when I jumped down, trying to hide the tears in my eyes as I looked at my battered glider, she took it from me and beckoned me to follow her. She fixed the glider, gluing it back together so well, that it looked like new. When I returned to Jimmy and the others, they told me to throw away the shortbread biscuit she had given me, in case she was trying to fatten me up, like the witch in 'Hansel and Gretel'. But it tasted so good, that I ate it anyway.

I hear two sets of soft-soled shoes approach and the man returns with a young nurse. He places a stainless steel bowl, half-filled with water, on the table. A drop splashes onto a silver picture frame. My eyes follow it as it rolls down the middle of the photo, dividing it in half. I squint and bend closer. It is a middle-aged couple. They are smiling into the camera. The man is tall with grey hair and blue eyes. The woman has chestnut brown hair, the same colour as her eyes.

The nurse picks up the photo and wipes the drop of water away, placing it back down in the exact same place. The glass is smeared and it is harder to make out the faces.

"We'll have you looking your best for Grace," says the nurse.

Grace must be important. They obviously want to impress her.

The rain is heavy now. The sky has turned slate grey and the trees are bending in the wind.

I feel something light and fluffy on my face. The man has a shaving brush in his hand. It has white bristles and a white square handle with black at the base. It reminds me of my father's. Jimmy and I loved to watch him as he shaved with such precision. He would rinse his brush in warm water and shake out the residue, sometimes flicking it at us. We would run, screaming from the room, with laughter. We would always return to watch, as he rubbed the brush round the creamy white soap in the black tub, before painting the lower half of his face. Sometimes, he let us try it too.

I can still smell the clean, fresh scent. Then he would open his stainless steel razor and bend close to the mirror. We would hold our breath, entranced, as he ran the razor down his face, leaving lines like railway tracks, before rinsing the blade and continuing on. When he was finished he would cup water in his huge hands and rinse his face before towelling dry. Then, he would pour a drop of Old Spice after shave into one hand, rub his hands together and pat them over his face. Most times he would pour, just the tiniest drop, into our waiting hands and we would do the same.

"There you go, Dan, much better," said the man, "oh, nearly forgot, just one last thing before I go!" He rubs his hands gently over my face. I inhale Old Spice. The man holds up the mirror again, "looking good, Dan." I see the same face looking back. But this time he is clean shaven and his eyes are now a watery blue.

The credits roll up the TV screen; Humphrey Bogart and Lauren Bacall. But I cannot recall the name of the film. They made so many films together; maybe it was . . . I turn my head, hearing the clip, clip sound of high heels coming closer. It is a brisk walk, like someone with a purpose.

They slow and a woman appears in the doorway, taking a pair of worn black leather gloves from her tiny hands as she enters. She has grey hair, cut into a neat bob. A blue coat clings to her thin frame, but it is the beautiful silk scarf tucked into her collar that catches my attention. It reminds me of the scarf Joe sent to mother. The same year Jimmy and—

"Hello Daniel," she says as she bends and kisses me on the mouth!

She squeezes my shoulders gently and looks into my eyes, "you look well today. And don't you smell nice, Old Spice," she says huskily, as she breathes in deeply and rubs the back of her fingers across my cheek.

Standing up straight, she gives a dry cough and shrugs off her coat. It smells damp. She drapes it over the back of the chair, places her umbrella on the floor at her feet and sits down. She rummages in her leather handbag and takes out a bulging, brown paper bag.

She pokes through its contents, extracts a cellophane wrapper and like a magician performing a magic trick, she pulls both ends to release a white iced caramel into my outstretched hand.

I gaze at it, turn it from side-to-side and examine it closely. I hold it close to my nose and sniff. It smells good. I feel my mouth water. I look up to see her watching me. My tongue darts out and licks the hard, sweet icing.

"Put it in your mouth, sweetheart" she says, as she plucks it from my hand and drops it into my open mouth.

She has a melodic voice. I wonder if she sings. It soothes me to listen to her. But I do not understand why she tells me stories of people I do not know.

As I suck, I feel it melt; toffee, sticky and chewy oozes out and I resist the urge to chew. Instead, I let it sit on my tongue until there is nearly nothing left. Only then do I chew, using my tongue to prise the remains from my teeth.

"This is nice, Daniel, nearly like old times; the pink for me and the white for you."

I hold my hand out and wait for another.

I notice her pink lipstick matches the splashes of pink in

her scarf. She has beautiful brown eyes, but they look tired and there are dark shadows beneath them. She looks vaguely familiar. I feel I may have seen her somewhere before.

The man returns with a plastic beaker, a mug of tea and a plate of shortbread biscuits.

"Well, doesn't he look nice today, Grace," he says, "all ready for your visit today."

So this is Grace.

She nods.

"Make sure you drink that tea. It'll help keep you warm on the journey home," he gestures towards the brown paper bag, "and if that's empty, I'll bin it for you."

It is no longer bulging.

"You're very kind, Brian," says Grace, squeezing the last of the wrappers inside and passing it to him. "How's Daniel doing?" she nods her head in my direction. I wonder why she does not ask me.

"He's having a good day, today. Watched one of his Bogart movie's earlier, didn't you Dan, you know the one—"

A porter comes into the ward waving a brass bell. The clanging sound announces the end of visiting time.

Grace stands up and puts on her damp coat, tucking her scarf around her neck before fastening the buttons.

"Goodbye Daniel," she whispers, as she kisses me on the mouth again, "I miss you."

She wipes a tear from her eye. I admire the light dancing from the diamond in her ring.

I remember Grace now. I knew I had seen her before.

I look up to catch her stare at me, her head to one side. I smile.

She is the woman in the silver picture frame, standing beside the grey-haired man with the blue eyes . . .

SEAMUS MCKENNA

Seamus McKenna's primary qualification is in Civil Engineering (ONC Civil Eng), which he obtained at Waterford Regional College, now South East Technological University. He holds an MBA from Trinity College, Dublin, a HNC in Computer Science from North West Regional College, Derry, and a Diploma in Accounting and Finance from the Association of Chartered Certified Accountants (Dip(A&F))

He is currently working for an MA in Creative Writing at Dublin City University (DCU).

A career that has taken him from his home town of Waterford initially to Donegal and Derry, NI, and later to Belgium and The Netherlands, with stints in Malaysia, has seen him involved in Engineering, Algorithmic Foreign Exchange trading, Business Analysis, and writing.

He is the author of The Omicron Forex Trading Manual (2012), which is available from Amazon.com and all its worldwide sites. See it here: https://www.amazon.com/Omicron-Forex-Trading-Manual/dp/1479247138

His blog, Stack Six, can be found at http://stacksix.blogspot.com/

He has been having his letters published periodically in the Irish Times since 1978.

He lives in Dublin with his wife, Marilyn. He has a son and a daughter, two granddaughters and one grandson.

A GAME FOR BISHOPS - SEAMUS MCKENNA

The first to arrive, two police people, a man and a woman, seemed to be rather affected by what they saw. Both became hysterical, in fact. It looked like it was only with difficulty that they were able to call for assistance. Then the place was full of their colleagues, and with ambulance people too. He heard one of the medics tell the police that they should go for counselling. He supposed there was a lot of blood alright, because there wasn't anywhere for it to go, unlike in the slaughterhouse where he had served his time. There, when it ran into the gullies that directed it to the storage tanks where it was saved to make black pudding, it was at least no longer visible. Out of sight, out of mind, you could say.

Also, the police would not have been accustomed to seeing organs that had been removed from a body that was alive a very short time ago. Those items still had steam rising from them as they lay there on the kitchen floor. His own shirt front was destroyed too, for that matter, and he could feel the goo on his chin and neck. It was impossible to wipe it off.

He had held on to the tools of his trade. He had a cleaver, a boning knife, a paring knife, and a fillet knife. He had a flensing knife, traditionally used in the whaling industry of old. These knives were very sharp. He also owned a butcher's saw. He was not afraid of the sight of blood. Perhaps he should have been a surgeon. Too late for that now, at any rate. His friends often asked him to bring along one of these knives when they wanted to carve a joint for a dinner party. He had arrived here tonight with one in the boot of his car, in a nice presentation case, because he had forgotten to remove it after the last time it was needed for something like that.

The weather was bad when he had set out. It was freezing in fact, and there were showers of sleet all along the way. There weren't too many other cars about when he had arrived at Dominick's house.

Dominick. Yes. Dominick and his accursed chess. Dominick's day job was as an insurance broker. He travelled around the city and county, using his people skills to induce the public to buy insurance. He must have been good at it, because he always seemed to have plenty of money. Some other members of the group had voiced the opinion that, maybe, Dominick might use his interaction with insurance clients to further their religious endeavours, but Dominick had rejected the idea. There was very little doubt that his employers would object to something like that, now that the godless liberal agenda was dominant.

Dominick was a large man, with a shape like the outer one of those Russian dolls that fit into one another: Matryoshka dolls. The lower part of his torso seemed to swell out, in a giant pear shape. He was not bald, but he didn't have much hair either. His was in his late thirties, but still single. He owned a house in a rather salubrious part of town, and it was there that most of their group meetings were held. This was the house he had grown up in, as an only child. His parents were now dead, but when they were alive, Dominick had told him, they had instilled in him a religious belief that had made him want to help others by bringing them to the core truth of their existence: the promise of eternal life through Jesus Christ.

Although they were Roman Catholic, they had found kindred spirits among the evangelical Christians in certain Mideast states, like Tennessee and Kentucky, when they had travelled to the United States. Dominick told him that these people were lovely. They had a nice sense of humour too. One of the families that his parents had stayed with in the US had a sticker on the back bumper of their car which said, in small writing: "If you can read this we have to ask: are you this close to Jesus?" They also did not drink alcohol too much. Although some of them had been divorced, the divorce rate amongst evangelical Christians in the US is significantly lower than it is among the general population.

They were aware of stories to the effect that some of the US evangelical preachers on TV had embezzled funds, or had carried on with women who were not their wives, but these cases were explained either by the well-known weaknesses inherent in human nature, or by the fact that they were downright false allegations that had been circulated by the secular main-stream press, which always had it in for good Christians.

The most important thing that Dominick told him about the American Christians was that they stood up for the same things that good Irish Catholics supported. They wanted a total ban on abortion, and they thought that marriage was something that could only be contracted between a man and a woman. Women could not change into men on a whim, or vice versa. Not only did they support these principles, but they worked hard to at least try to make sure that the laws of the land reflected their policies in these matters. It was a pity that governments here had lost sight of that imperative.

The group to which they both belonged came together for prayer and meditation and, frankly, to ponder how they might enlarge their circle. They saw themselves as something of an elite group, although they were not rebels. Not at all. They adhered to Catholic doctrine, and if they made any kind of a wave, it was to ensure that their nominal co-religionists stayed as close as possible to official Vatican teaching. All believed that there were far too many à la carte Catholics around nowadays, people who picked and chose what they wanted from their church, which often had the effect of making it more of a social group than a religion. One of the members had come up with a new expression to describe those Catholics who had maintained their allegiance, it seemed, for the sole purpose of allowing their children, and themselves, to enjoy the social occasion that First Holy Communion had become. These were now to be called Bouncy Castle Catholics. This was a clever play on the term given to those Irish people who were prepared to work with the British administration at Dublin Castle before independence, who were known as Castle Catholics.

When Dominick had suggested that they play chess in the times when they were not praying and contemplating, or discussing theological matters, he had not realised that the big guy was so good at it. Then Dominick had tried to teach him. His protestation that he did not need to be taught, that he had been playing chess for a long time, and with good success, fell on deaf ears.

"Don't bring out your queen too soon," Dominick would say. Yes, right, he knew about that. He also knew how to play, and react to, the Sicilian Defence. He knew that he should castle as soon as possible, and that his rooks, while remaining on the back rank, should be connected, or able to support each other without any intervening pieces, after about thirteen or fourteen moves had been played. He knew that he should practice making a careful examination of the board before each move to make sure that he did not leave a piece hanging, or exposed to capture without a return, by ensuring that its square was protected by one of his other pieces, or at least not within reach of one of Dominick's killers: his knights, which were insidious, with their complicated up and across moves; or a bishop that could lie in wait, ready to discharge itself like a sniper with a high-powered rifle when it saw a victim, from behind a hedge of pawns and from about as far away as it was possible to be on the board. Not being able to beat Dominick at chess was frustrating, for sure. No matter how he practiced, no matter how much he read up on the subject, Dominick still came out on top, and always accompanied his wins with advice. Dominick was God when he played chess. He wanted to be like Dominick.

The theological debates centred on Catholic matters, although he was aware that theology was the study of God in general. It derived from the Greek words Theos, which meant God, and logos, meaning learning, and therefore could have taken in other religions. Even here Dominick insisted on telling him things he already knew, such as that those who partook of the Eucharist in communion were eating the person of Christ. The wafer was not something that represented Christ's flesh; it was Christ's flesh. According to James Anthony Froude, a member of the so-called Oxford movement, which was probably closer to Catholicism than it was to the official Church of England, this had a rising and filling effect upon believers, so that Christ spread throughout their beings, their souls, in the manner of a leavening agent in baked bread. This meant that the more you ate of the body of Christ in Communion, the more like Christ you became. Christlike. Yes.

They had prayed, as usual, after he had arrived. They should have been joined by two other people, but neither of them could come because of the weather conditions. Then they had the discussion on theology. He was, also as usual, impressed by Dominick's learning, and his confidence in his knowledge. He specialised in Biblical Theology, which was the alternative to Historical Theology; there was nothing he did not know about the subject. He wished he was like Dominick in this area too.

He knew that there was also a body of study on Islam. By rights, that should be Theology too. The five pillars. Right up at the top was the profession of faith. All religions demanded that. Then prayer. Nothing strange there; his and Dominick's religion also had prayer. Giving alms was important to the Muslims, and all of Christianity had its charitable institutions, of course. There was fasting. We used to do that during Lent, but Ramadan is far more real for Muslims than the kind of Lenten observation we follow in modern times. Lastly, there was pilgrimage. Sure, Catholics liked to go to Rome, and to the Marion shrines at Lourdes, Knock, Fatima, and Medjugorje, but none of them had the level of obligation that a visit to Mecca had for a Muslim. Every Muslim who had health, and who could afford it, must make at least one visit to Mecca during their lifetime.

They had a cup of tea and some cakes, which was the normal fare. Dominick was anything but stingy, although other members always brought along some little thing; nobody felt good about coming with their hands hanging. But no alcoholic drink. Of any kind. There was enough bitterness and division in society already because of the drink.

Then it was time for chess. Dominick allowed him to play white, although it wasn't his turn. That looked just a little bit like condescension. Was he being patronised? He set up the board: white on the right, which meant that the farthest square on the right of the board, as seen by each player, was a white square. Then the queens were put on their own colour squares, with the kings beside them in such a way that the royal couple's bodies took up the middle squares of the back rank for each player. After that the hierarchy of bishop, knight and rook took their places out to left and right on each side from the king and queen. For each player a row of eight pawns was placed in front of the major pieces.

Then they began to play.

He moved his king pawn two squares forward. Dominick did the same. They both brought out one knight. He moved one of his bishops. He knew that this meant they had the Italian game underway, which is one of the oldest openings.

But it all went downhill for him from there on. He just couldn't focus enough to be sure that he had no hanging pieces, and Dominick swooped whenever he saw that happening. And it happened at lot. He never seemed to be able to spot any mistakes of this kind that Dominick had made. They hadn't even reached what could be called an endgame when he rose from his chair.

"Dominick," he said, "I have to go out to the car to get something."

A SHARED SPACE - SEAMUS MCKENNA

Fighting words workshop DCU 23rd February 2023

1

Brace decided he'd return home on the other side of the river. The place was getting quieter; there was a noticeable reduction in the number of people about, either on foot or on a bike. But that alone might make it easier to catch sight of a kingfisher.

After walking some way along the path, he realised that coming home this way might not have been the best idea. The trees were denser. They shut out a lot of the daylight, of the little that was left. His feet squelched underfoot on the slippery mass of wet leaves. The path was on two levels, like giant steps. The part closest to the river was the top of a concrete embankment, and the walkway that he was on was about half the height of a person above that.

It was an overcast day, and cold with it. This was mid-winter, after all; the kind of January day that we are told plays hell with those of a vulnerable mental disposition.

Still no kingfisher, but he did see a heron, standing in the middle of the river, on top of the noisy weir.

Might as well get a photo of that.

He took out his smartphone and crouched to get a good view. That was a mistake. He felt his feet slide from under him. Then he was throwing himself to his right to avoid falling onto the concrete embankment. He managed that but at the cost of letting go of his phone, which landed on the lower level. Then his leg twisted, and he heard a snap. The pain that accompanied that was extreme. He knew at once that he had broken a bone.

He lay there for a minute or two, on his right-hand side,

feeling foolish as much as anything else. That was until he tried to move, when the pain took over. It was so intense that it caused him to scream, which was something he never did. Recovering his phone from the lower level was out of the question. He could see it alright, but to recover it would have been a hard job even without a broken leg.

Now it was getting quite dark. There was nothing else for it: he would have to call for help. And at the top of his voice.

"*Help…help…healp.*"

He realised he was competing with the noise from the weir. Not only that, the weir was winning. It was drowning out his cries. Christ it was cold. He couldn't move to get any circulation going; if he moved as much as a muscle, he suffered an agony from his leg.

Then he saw the screen of his mobile phone lighting up; it must be on the upside, and unbroken. That was probably his wife calling to see where he was. He could not hear the ring tone, although he knew the phone was not on silent. The screen stayed lit for some time, and then went off. How long before she would realise that his not answering meant he was in trouble?

He took a deep breath and called out again.

"*Heaalp. heelp…help.*"

His voice was getting squeaky. How long before he would be hoarse? The discomfort borne of the way he was lying was serious. So was the pain from his leg whenever he made the slightest effort to find any kind of a better position.

The darkness had taken over completely. There was no public lighting along the river, on either side.

"*Help…healp…help.*"

Time was passing. Brace could feel he was getting weaker. He had a good jacket, but it would not be protection against hypothermia, especially when he was constrained to lie motionless in this low temperature.

The screen on his phone lit up once more. Jennifer must be getting concerned, because he always answered.

2

"What I wouldn't give to see a kingfisher." Brace was reading the paper.

"What brought that on?"

"There's a picture of one here. Taken down on the Dodder. It says that they're very hard to see because they're tiny, and because they've learned to sit stock still so that they'll have the best chance of catching a fish."

"Well, the Dodder River is only down the road from here."

Brace suspected she was also thinking that it might get him out of the house for a while. He had been retired for over a year, and sometimes he might well have gotten under her feet at home.

"I'm going to go for a walk."

"Make sure to bring your umbrella, there's a forecast of rain."

He did, and he made sure to wrap up well.

A walk along the Dodder was going to be interesting in itself. As he left the public road and joined the path through the grassed area leading to the river, he walked past the children's playground.

NO ADULTS ALLOWED UNLESS ACCOMPANIED BY A CHILD

Brace was in his late-fifties, fit, and in good health. He had all his hair and all but two or three of his original teeth. He was just under six feet tall. He knew that when he stood up straight, he could be an imposing figure.

The path beside the river brought him past the remnants of an old mill race which, he had been told, was used many years ago to harness the energy of the river to power one of the two mills that had given that part of Dublin, Milltown, its name. The red brick chimney of one of those mills is still to be seen, alongside the Nine Arches Bridge, another imposing structure. This was once part of the Harcourt Street railway out of the city, and it now carries the modern LUAS tramline.

The footpath through the grassed area had a white line in the centre of it, which was supposed to separate walking and cycling areas. An impossible task, he thought, as families tended to walk in sizeable groups containing many children. But it was uncanny alright how one, mid-sized, dog walked along that white line. It kept all its paws on it, like a tight rope walker; there was no deviation whatever until the line petered out when the path reached the Dundrum Road.

After he had joined this path, he became aware of a group of two women and three children in front of him. A mature man on a bike came along. Then he was ringing his bell at one of the children, who had wandered out in front of him. Brace saw red. He rushed forward and confronted the cyclist.

"You have no right to ring your bell at that child," he said. "This is not a cycle path."

The rider scowled.

"There's a white line here for dividing it into cycling and walking lanes."

"That can only be a suggestion. This was always a footpath and the best that you can say about it now is that it's a shared space."

Brace kept his rolled-up umbrella pressed into his side. He did not want to be accused of assaulting this person.

The cyclist stood up on his pedals and made off.

The women in the group thanked him for his intervention. This made him self-conscious, almost embarrassed.

A little further on he walked over the abutment of the

ancient pack-horse bridge, which had been part of the road out of Dublin until the construction of Glasson's Bridge a little downstream, and the more recent Milltown bridge a little upstream. Pack-horse bridges were narrow, so were designed with low parapet walls to allow horses loaded with panniers, or containers on the horse's side, to cross them.

All of this would be even more interesting if it weren't for all the people bringing their dogs, large and small, for a walk. Well, the people walked, the large dogs bounded, often chasing tennis balls that had been thrown by their humans.

And don't mention the cyclists. Large road bikes which, their mass combined with that of a grown man, and travelling at speeds that came close to the limit for motor vehicles, would have built up a level of kinetic energy, he knew, that was enough to cause serious injury to any pedestrian they collided with. That part of the story was downright dangerous.

One summer, passing this spot, he had been noticed by a woman as he bent to appreciate the scent from some hedgerow plants that grew there, without plucking them. She smiled. Did she smile at the idea of a guy being interested in something like that? He was reminded of the reaction of one of his female acquaintances, Margaret, when he related his experience, on one occasion, with a lorry salesman.

"My brother and I were in a lorry dealer's yard looking for parts. We noticed a small truck, with large numbers, both in size and in value, planted on the front. My brother knew enough about this make to realise that those numbers were not original equipment.

"What's that about?" they had asked the yard owner.

"Oh, those numbers. Well, the guy who traded that in had a driver who was always getting slagged in the pub because his truck was so small. Other truckers would say to him that the vehicle he had was only a Dinky, hahaha. My customer wanted to do something for him, so I got those big numbers and riveted them onto the front of the cab."

"And did that do the trick?"

"Absolutely, there was never a word of complaint from the driver after that."

That pleased Margaret.

"Fellas," she was able to say, "are so stupid."

On the right as he progressed was the single Shi'a Muslim mosque in all of Ireland, north and south. He knew there were many Sunni Mosques, but this one was the sole mosque dedicated to the use of the Shi'a sect.

Then he crossed the Dundrum Road, to bring him to the continuation of the Dodder path on the other side. No sign of a kingfisher, but there was a brace of mallard ducks there, both browsing. And more dogs. Ducks are not unusual at all on the Dodder, but sometimes people are delighted to see Mandarin Ducks, which are brightly coloured, with complex facial and body feathers that are reminiscent, right enough, of Chinese art. According to Eithne Viney in the Irish Times, these exotic creatures established themselves in the Dodder after a number of them escaped from a private collection. It was lucky for us that this happened, and that they were able to survive and procreate in the Irish climate. No sign of any of them today, however.

Those fucking dogs, and their humans. He once saw a pair of canines tearing along a shallow part of the river in pursuit of ducks, all the while being encouraged by a person who was, presumably, supposed to be in charge of them. He imagined that the ducks would have made themselves very scarce in that part of the river for a long time after that. Such ignorance and stupidity on the part of the human, all leading to a diminution of the enjoyment that other people get from the river.

He passed a low part of the riverbank where, in season, he

often saw people fishing. This was not the season, however; it was the very depths of winter. Already the daylight was beginning, ever so slightly, to fade. He also found himself pulling the collar of his jacket closer around his neck.

There is a weir on this part of the river. The water tumbling over it made quite a bit of noise. The fish had no difficulty in negotiating it, apart from the risk of being caught by a heron. Now he could see one of those birds at the entrance to a small tributary of the river, standing stock-still, waiting for its opportunities. Once he had seen one catch a fish. The prey was rather large for the bird. It kept escaping, and then being recaptured. After this had happened on about four occasions, Brace was so frustrated that he felt like shouting, "throw it up on to the bank!". That would have been possible, and he wondered why such birds had not evolved the habit of doing so; nature and evolution had made them pretty smart in other respects. He scoured the area around the heron for any sign of a kingfisher. There was nothing to be seen. Do they compete for areas in which to operate?

The women and children were still a little in front of him; he and they seemed to be walking at the same pace.

There was no frost underfoot, but plenty of saturated dead leaves, which made the path slippery. And squelchy. There was moss also, but he reckoned that was a leftover from a warmer season of the year.

Here and there a bench seat had been erected in memory of a departed individual who, the brass plate often said, had enjoyed his or her walks along this very path. How poignant. These were substantial structures, with good concrete foundations, all made to the same design. The County Council must put them up in return for a payment from the families of the dead person.

A rolled-up umbrella with a hooked handle was your only

man for walking. He couldn't understand how people took golf umbrellas, with their straight handles, when they went strolling. Now he was able to amble along like the man with the silver handled walking stick he had encountered promenading along Piccadilly in London all those years ago. That gentleman had nodded to him in greeting, even though they had been total strangers. Perhaps this was down to the feeling of bonhomie he associated with the image of a gentlemen strolling along Piccadilly with the assistance of a silver handled walking stick. He emulated that man now, swinging his rolled-up umbrella to the rhythm of his walk.

He continued to scan the river for the elusive kingfisher. He wondered would he have a better chance of seeing it if he was down lower, as close as possible to the level of the water? The river was moving at a reasonable pace, not turbulent, but not tranquil either.

One of the children in the group up ahead, a little boy, would have been aged between two and three, little more than a toddler. The woman who seemed to be his mother wheeled an empty stroller buggy, perhaps in case he got tired. But he was quite lively, with a good interest in all the things around him. He seemed to be a happy, intelligent child, with a sense of inquiry, which Brace thought delightful, and was all the time babbling away in his baby language. His hair was pitch black, and of strong growth. The adults gave him plenty of attention.

The group had reached the break in the wall that separated the Dodder walk from the Clonskeagh road.

Then Brace was shocked to see the expression on the little boy's face change to one of sheer terror. Later he thought it was hard to believe that such strong emotion could be displayed by one so young. The reason became clear: a large, dun coloured dog had appeared beside the child. It had, up to then, been obscured by the wall. The dog was reaching for the by now frantic boy's head. Brace got a firm hold of his rolled-up umbrella and rushed forward. He aimed blow after blow at the dog's snout, just in front of its eyes. The animal yelped, and took flight. Then there was a flurry during which the child was taken by his mother into her arms, and the owner of the dog came up onto the scene.

"What the fuck do you think you're doing to my dog?"

"Your stupid dog was attacking a child."

"The dog is young. She only wanted to play with the child. She does that at home all the time."

"The child is traumatised. Does that not mean anything to you? And your dog should be on a lead. I think I should call the police"

"That won't be necessary." The owner bent to attach a lead to the dog's collar.

Brace's concern now was the little boy.

"How is he?" he asked the mother.

"I think he'll be all right. Thanks again."

Brace moved to the side of the Madonna tableau so that he could look into the boy's face. He thought he detected a hint of a smile, in between sobs. That made him feel a little less angry.

3

Must not fall asleep or pass out. That could be fatal. There had been stories of people being discovered dead from hypothermia in similar conditions. It was ironic that in a lot of those cases drink had been involved; he would never come down here if he was drunk.

The pain had eased, but only a little. Any movement was still impossible.

He was somewhat dazed when he heard a rustling of the drier leaves above him, away from the river path.

He found his voice again.

"*Heaalp. heeelp…help.*"

Then his face was being touched by the cold nose of a large dog. It sniffed him all over. He craned his neck as far as he could, which was not far, to see if an owner or handler was close. He couldn't see anyone.

Then the dog raced off.

Time to start shouting again, as much as he could. His phone lit up again, and stayed that way for the longest time.

When it dimmed, he drew in his breath for another bout of calling for help. He wasn't sure what he sensed next, the light that approached him, or the rustling of the drier leaves. But then there was a man standing over him with a bright lamp on the handlebars of a bicycle.

"Are you all right?"

"I have a broken leg, I think. I can't move at all."

"Right. I'll phone for an ambulance. I know nothing about First Aid, but I do have a phone."

He could hear the stranger telling the emergency services the story. There was the back and forth of a discussion for a minute or two and then, when he was finished, he said:

"Have you been here long?"

"Long enough. My phone fell down onto the ledge below. I couldn't get it back because I broke my leg."

"There will be an ambulance on the other side of the river shortly. They'll call me when they arrive and I'll shine the light of the bike to let them know where we are. I don't know what will happen then, but they'll probably be able to stretcher you out."

Brace's phone lit up again.

"That will be my wife. She must be very worried at this stage. Would it be possible for me to use your phone to call her?"

"Of course."

When that call had been made, much to the relief and delight of Brace's wife, the stranger said:

"You're very lucky. My dog disappeared for a while and when she came back, she was very excited. I tried to put the lead on her, because it was long past time for us to go home. It was dark except for the light of the stars and probably some distant street lights, but she wouldn't let me put it on. She ran around in circles, barking, some of the time moving away in this direction. Then I realised she wanted me to follow her. She led me here."

"And you had the light on your bike to show the way."

"That's right. It's a beautiful machine. A very light aluminium frame. It's very easy to ride in a woodland area like this. I was able to keep up with my dog."

Brace thought again of dogs and bikes along the river Dodder walk.

A FACE

Aye, there are a few wrinkles there all right, mainly at the outsides of the eyes. Some people call these crow's feet. The eyebrows arch quite strongly from where they start at the top of the nose, but then level out before disappearing altogether, long before they reach the other side of each eye. There's a strong nose, nicely shaped, with smooth channels on each side, starting at the fleshy part about the nostrils and curving down to touch the sides of the mouth. Medium high cheekbones serve to highlight the actual cheeks. One feature of this face that would have to be noted by an artist or sketcher is the distance between the hinges of the jaw. Said artist would be constrained to draw an almost vertical line from the ears down to a position just below the mouth, and then fairly quickly turn in on each side to attack the small cleft in the chin. The mouth is a perfect cupid's bow, with lips that are nicely formed, neither too full nor too thin. There is only a suggestion of a philtrum, that vertical channel between the nose and the upper lip. The form of the mouth is almost, but not quite, symmetrical around its horizontal centre. Apparently the ancient Greeks regarded this to be a very sensual feature, when present. Then there is the colouring: she likes to sunbathe but is careful about not getting too much exposure, and it shows. Her eyes are blue, and have always maintained the penetrating aspect to which he was so attracted from the start. The lips, of course, can change their colour, depending on the lipstick that she chooses to wear on a given day. The same goes for the hair, that perfectly maintained frame for the subject of this piece, that face.

A VISIT TO A GRANDMOTHER

"Hello Seamus."

"I was told I was wanted in the office."

"Yes. We've just had a phone call. Your grandmother has taken a turn for the worse. They think you should go and see her."

"OK. She hasn't been well. I'm going to need some time off then."

"That's fine. Compassionate leave. Off you go."

Her bed was surrounded by his cousins, aunts and uncles when he got there. He could only find a space at the bottom, and he had to remain standing.

"I must be on the way out now. You've never all come to see me at the same time before. Some of you haven't even come to see me on your own."

"She's a tough woman."

"Yes, she always was. Right from when she was a young one and marched with all the other women in Kilkenny to sign the petition against conscription in 1918. It can still be seen, with her signature in it, in the Kilkenny Archaeological Society."

"That's not the half of it. If you study it carefully you'll see that she went back three or four times with a few of her friends to sign it multiple times."

"Or when your grandfather died after being kicked by an ass. She had to raise your father, your aunt and your three uncles on her own. With no income. She took on a job selling insurance."

"They had a bit of land, didn't they?"

"A very small piece, with no water. And to make it worse, her barn with all her hay in it was burnt just after the foundation of the state. She got no compensation for that. She was on the side of the Blueshirts. The whole family was."

"There was bitter division in Ireland at that time."

"The story of her life is the story of Ireland."

AFTER PROUST

He did not hear it often, but when he did, the bock-bagawking of chickens, no matter where in the world he was, brought him back, as vividly as if he were physically transported there, to the yard outside his mother's home place where he used to spend every summer until he was five. Then other memories would arrive; of walking through the garden of blackberry bushes at the side of the house, which, relative to his childframe, he perceived to be of enormous size but, when visited in adult life, proved to have an unexceptional scale, of even being small; of being brought by his aunt Julia, by the hand, to pick nettles for nettle soup. He had memory neither of picking the nettles nor of eating the soup, only of being informed by that lady that it was to carry out those activities that they were bound when they set off; of his grandfather and his uncle Jack cutting timber, later to be chopped up for firewood, on the other side of the lane, with a cross-cut saw. One or other of the adults would light the Tilley-lamps in the evening, and it was not until he moved to a modern house, in his sixth year of age, that he realised that switching on an electric light was not a facility that they possessed. Aunt Julia baked both brown and white soda bread every day, in a big black pot that hung down from the chimney over a fire of turf and timber that never went out; it was allowed to go down to its lowest when everyone had gone to bed, and was revived the next morning by the simple expedient of adding more fuel. They milked a single cow, and Julia kept two goats that he realised, even at that young age, were her special responsibility.

ANDY MACKEN

Andy draws on his Dublin background , family histories and personal stories for his writing. A lecture by Anne Enright inspired him to write and he has recently completed an MA in Creative Writing at Dublin City University while continuing his day job as an Architect.

He is working on his first book, a collection of short stories, Lion's Manes and Pintails, tales of Dubliners and the sea. He lives in Kilmainham with his husband and children and swims in Dublin Bay.

HOMECOMING - ANDY MACKEN

We are creating our 'forever home', and it may just take us forever. Still a house of drafty floors and doors, swirly carpets, still cramped and awkward in parts. Ours will be a home both bright and light, understated, solid and safe.

We are still early, on this uphill journey to the heavenly bright and light goal. The ground floor is our level playing field, much achieved with our new zinc and glass box to the rear. An expanse of travertine and our streamlined walnut blocks of kitchen cabinetry make the point for our modernity but all this newness, this 'us' with a view beyond to the builder's yard that is our back garden reveals our state of flux. The battle for ownership is now being fought in the hall, stairs and landing, where century old dado rails, fixed above fans of combed plaster are slowly and painstakingly – by my tired hands - revealing lime scrub plaster. Yet for now I must run down my maternity freedom days in this decaying Victoriana.

Much more to do upstairs. The former home from another era still exists, with it came the grungiest of bathrooms. This room is tired of life, with its high cistern loo and strafed old chrome mirror, a washstand that brings to mind, preening ladies with their victory rolls and up-dos, surrounded by cracked tiles of yellows and blues of a different time. A pleasant-looking cast iron bathtub stands almost centre stage, with copper flecked lion's feet and faded enamel, no longer white. The heavy-duty brass mixer sits tall and ladylike on the deep rim, and it is here we find ourselves in the quiet time after breakfast, sundrenched in morning light.

My flaxen-haired cherub, all shiny sudsy and pink of cheek. Her perfect toothless mug, beaming with full flourish, loving her morning bathing ritual. The younger mums from the baby group tell me not to bathe her every day, but I'll do whatever sustains me from not returning to bed after her Daddy has left for the day. We settle into our cycle of breakfast, bathe, play and planning our endless downtime.

Today we have a welcome distraction. I notice a stranger on the pavement below slowly walking up our path. Not the greyhound lean postman, someone new. In the sunlight this golden-haired stranger with tanned features and expensive leather coat is positively beamed in from another planet. I watch him approach the porch and almost forget to think what his business might be.

He's writing a note, and he has a companion, a younger woman, she has stayed back across the road and signals to my window as she looks up. I hesitate and retreat behind the curtain, then go to the top of the stairs and wait for the bell to go but it doesn't ring. After a pause the letter box gives a clatter. As I crouch down on the landing, I can see his dark outline and fair head through the frosted glass, but he pauses – a respectful distance and outside the porch by my calculation – but doesn't move.

There's a slip of paper now on the tiled floor, just inside the front door. Child in arms, I descend the stairs and see his figure is gone. I pick up the note and open the door to check and see that the man is still there. He is, at the end of the garden path, waiting, unsure.

'Hello,' he says carefully, I'm clearly startled, not expecting him to still be there. I look down at the open note in my hand and notice blocky handwriting and pick out the word 'adopted'.

With polite hesitation he walks back up the path and I notice the woman is still there and smiling at me, reassuring. I also notice the man is strikingly handsome, and tall, rugby build. I imagine he is older than me. Handsome in the face, rugged, too much sun on that chiseled jawline. Much older than the woman he came with.

He takes a breath and explains the content of the note.

He has been to Liverpool and was given an address in Dublin to find.

'My mother lived here, she went to Liverpool, I was born there'.

Adding, 'this was her address, her home'.

His accent is hard to place.

'I've come from Australia,' he explains.   Accent and purpose clarified.   I step down on the path and he almost whispers a woman's name, his eyes suggesting this is a question.

I'm looking at him and acknowledging with a nod the name, his mother's name, as he explains she lived here for most of her life.

This is the name of the woman we bought the house from, but I carefully and quietly explain we never met her as she had moved into a nursing home, we dealt with an agent.

'It was a few years back,' I add, and then stop, as with sudden horror I remember being told she had died some time ago.

For a moment I squint in the sun and try to see if he knows this fact, but it's quickly established that he does. And I breathe a sigh of relief as I don't have the unenviable task of providing this piece of news myself.

'Look, this might sound a bit nuts, but you mind if I were to see the house at some point,' he asks politely adding 'maybe later at a time that suits? It's just I know she lived here from birth until she went into care,' I note a touch of pleading in his tone.

There is a heavy pause as they watch me cycle through the options, but the baby gurgles her approval and I relent, it's the right thing to do, he seems safe, female companion for safety.

'It's fine,' I say. He offers his hand and introduces himself and I lead the way through the porch. The woman announces she will wait outside, when she prepares to light a cigarette, I don't protest. So just the two of us.

This is a nice, decent thing to do, and he is deeply satisfying to look at. Well dressed. Tasteful silver wedding band. Glorious head of hair. Plausible reasoning.

Leading him into the lounge and making my excuses I go through to the kitchen to put the baby down.

I come back to him, offering tea or coffee, but he gives a 'thanks, but no thanks'. He asks if his mother left anything in the house, but I hand motion and say 'just the fixtures'. He starts to talk.

He runs off the details, she was born in Dublin and lived with her family in this house. She was the only child. He runs through a story I've heard before, she was a teenager, pregnant, not married and was sent away to England. He states his birth year, twelve years my senior, I note.

'She had to give me up, and I was adopted and brought to Oz for life in the sun, but she came back here. I am guessing she probably had no choice.'

He looks tender and breaks eye contact, glancing across the old mantelpiece, heavily laden with images of my family life. The same old mantelpiece would have seen his mother through almost all of her life, but not a life that involved her son. I suggest we take a tour.

He makes approving noises as I walk and talk him through our downstairs past, present and future works and note he has stopped at the garden window, staring transfixed at something in the general rubble out back. I follow his gaze to the old scullery fire surround laid flat; its flowery ceramic tiles set out on the ground like a smashed jigsaw.

I offer, 'it was a fireplace, ceramic, but we broke it during the works, trying to piece it back together, clumsy accident.' I sound excessively apologetic. He looks crestfallen over my tale of antique destruction. I stop warbling, suddenly conscious of my homeowner status.

Our tour moves through the downstairs and to the bottom of the staircase and I find myself embarrassed at the dilapidated state of the hallway. We creak up the old stairs, his hand caressing the chipped and unsanded handrail. The floor gives a groan as we reach the landing, and I can hear a cry from the kitchen. I nod to him to go ahead and quick step it back to the kitchen leaving him alone.

I settle her back to sleep in the kitchen and, coffee in hand, I look to the ceiling and listen to his heavy steps above. Is he imagining these rooms of old, with a young woman who finds herself staring at the walls of repeating roses, pacing those brown and orange swirls, pondering her options or lack thereof. Decisions made for her by others, perhaps.

The footfall has ceased, and I stop to listen - silence. At the bottom of the stairs I stop to work out where he is. All is quiet. I cautiously take it step by step as I creep up to the half landing where I am eye level with his polished brogue, he is in the bathroom.

I softly push the door open and see he is seated, on the edge of the bath, his head a corona of blonde hair, illuminated by the blast of mid-morning sun, as fair as a child. He is looking down into the old tub, his palm runs tenderly along the cast iron surface.

'She would have had her bath here,' he says, looking up, moist-eyed and vulnerable. For one long still moment we look at each other, locked in understanding and bathed in the sunlight, brilliant and warm.

The moment is broken with a ding from the tub as he

wraps his ringed hand on the enamel of the tub, stands up, offers a blustery thank you.

We return downstairs, and I open the door. The woman is waiting and greets him on the path.

'OK, Dad?' she asks, giving his back a circular rub.

He gives her a nod of appreciation and same back to me.

I have a thought that I can pass him on something tangible from this house, his mother's house no less.

'Just a minute,' I touch him on the forearm indicating he wait. They wait as I go back inside.

Returning a moment later, I pass an almost complete tile from the smashed fireplace into his hand. He looks down at the cracked glazed object, and then back at me with what seems to be real heartfelt appreciation, this has made my day.

They ask, so I take their photograph. Father and daughter, blonde and smiling, framed by the decorative brick of the porch. The one-time porch of his mother, her grandmother, no less. They say their goodbyes. I see her arm slips around his waist as they walk back towards the village.

Closing the heavy old front door, I make my way back to my sleeping baby. Fingers tracing along the walls, across the glazed surface of the undulating plaster grooves. Grooves someone had applied by hand, with great care, a long time ago.

ALEX GOMEZ HOYAS

Alex Gomez is a bilingual aspiring writer who has been told he's "great at English, for a Spanish person" repeatedly since he was 10 years old. After making it his lifelong, rage-fuelled commitment to outperform English speakers in their own language, it seems that spite has become genuine fondness and now he spends his time writing like his life is on the line.

He has a shiny certificate to account for the four years

devoted to his degree in English literature and linguistics, during which he published some academic essays and creative works in the Complutense University of Madrid journal JACLR. Immediately after graduating - and completely contrary to everyone's advice - he jumped straight into a creative writing MA in DCU, where he continued to experiment with the craft.

While his fiction typically features blends of fantasy and science fiction in vivid, colourful world building, his poetry is often rooted in the real world and addresses delicate themes of mental health, politics, and discrimination with a heavy tongue-in-cheek bite. He has a passion for travelling but hates getting out of bed and has willingly worked customer service in his never-ending quest to hear other people's stories. His current employment is in the healthcare sector, but he aspires to put all of his eclectic experience together as a screenwriter one day.

The short story here enclosed has nothing to do with any of the above except that it was written when our author was at the very end of his rope. It is in those moments when it doesn't matter how much we know or all that we've done because nothing takes away the feeling of our brains bursting- in those moments, we tell stories, because it is the only way to reclaim reality.

BILLY AND THE SEA - ALEX GOMEZ HOYAS

It started as a joke. It was never supposed to go that far, honest. Billy was new, so it made sense to play with him a bit. Animals do it too, give the new arrival a bit of hell to build camaraderie and such.

We'd all of us been working on the beach for at least a couple of years when he came in. He was an odd fellow and we knew it right off the bat – his eyes shone too much with eagerness, the kind you see in children or dogs, and he didn't walk places but seemed to bounce or skip to them. He smiled a lot, at all of our salt-worn faces with his fresh cheeks. It was Lolo who suggested what we did.

"Hey, Billy. Bill."

Getting Billy's attention was easy, he seemed to hear you no matter how quietly you called his name. Like he secretly wanted you to say it and he was constantly expectant, hoping against hope that now would be the minute where someone needed him.

"Yeah?" said Billy, smiling his acknowledgement with his whole dumb, honest face. "What's it? You all right?"

Some of us, I admit, sniggered, waiting to see Lolo in action. It was harmless fun for us. Just a joke to put his effortless glow to the test.

"Yeah, fine," said Lolo, and then put on a very serious face and he walked up to Billy and touched him, circling his shoulders with an arm. "But we've got a problem. See there, the sea keeps taking away the sand. It does it every day, and it makes it hard to keep the beach nice."

Billy hummed, nodding along, wide eyes on the everlasting ocean winking foam back. Like he'd never seen it before, silly oaf, and had never noticed the sand thin with the backwash.

Someone nudged me in the side and I did the same back, subtle as I could, but I don't think it would have mattered because Billy was absorbed in the problem Lolo was posing to him.

We were too far to hear it from his mouth at the time, because he lowered his voice to keep it intimate, like. Making Billy think he was the only one in on it. But Lolo told us later and it basically went like this:

"We need you to protect the sand there, good man. You need to keep the sea from taking it. We all do our best too, but we really need your help on this."

I have to say, none of us expected Billy to take it seriously, but then again all of us had been on that beach for years. We knew all too well that there was nothing one single man could do to stave off the sea and keep the sand intact. It was just the way the sea was, it came, it went, it stole a part of the beach away. We never guessed Billy might not get it since it was so obvious to us. But Billy was young, and besides he had been here very little time. He didn't know these things, and Lolo gave him the impression that he stood a chance. That it wasn't as pointless as it might sound.

So imagine our surprise when we left him there that Wednesday after our shift, and when we got back next morning we were notified we'd be one pair of hands short. Apparently the idiot had stood there, in that same patch of sand, all night, furiously trying to shield it with his feet and his arms. They found him half-drowned and hypothermic come daytime and sent him to spend that day in medical.

Some of us were a little nervous, but we laughed. All of us laughed actually, some nervous, like I said, some at the sheer absurdity of it. We expected that would be that, someone would tell him it was a silly quest, a job-warming joke if you will, and that would be the end of it. There was never malice in it. We really thought he'd know better by the time he returned to us. It came as a shock to everyone that his next shift, he did the exact same thing.

Billy lost two fingers that time, to frostbite. He kept his hands in the water the whole night. Apparently he thought he'd made a mistake before, in pulling his hands out of the sea when he got cold. He thought he just had to hold on through it. We were told it was a miracle he'd made it through the night.

They questioned us a bit, asking us where those ideas had come from. It was a sobering talk, realising we were partly to blame, and even more so when we saw him next time, down two fingers. I myself had never seen anyone missing any body parts except maybe teeth. It was enough to make me a little sick, deep in my stomach. It put me off my lunch that day, and the next. I tried not to look at him very much. The rest were probably feeling a bit like that too, because we all got a little cold around Billy. We were ashamed, I think, though we probably didn't know it then.

There was no way Billy could have known that either. The idiot thought we were angry at him – he said it, out loud. He apologised to us. Said he got that we were disappointed at his miserable fumbling with the task we'd set out for him.

Most of us were a little aghast at this, to the point we were annoyed, but Lolo most of all. Management had spoken to him the longest and he wasn't happy about it right now.

"Listen here, you stupid creature, just forget about it. You were never going to win."

The words he said didn't really match what he meant, which all of us but Billy understood. What Lolo really meant was that Billy should stop trying because there was no 'quest'. It was an impossible task, a joke. He was admitting his wrong in teasing him. All of us felt that. We all got it, because we felt that way too but it would have been much too hard to say it like that, so Lolo's words came as much from his gut as they came from ours. We're not the first to dress up complicated nonsense like guilt and shame as anger, which is much simpler, and I tell you we definitely won't be the last.

Billy, though... Billy didn't work that way. He didn't dress up his feelings as others, so we all saw the hurt, then the determination. There was something a little feverish in the way he shook his head.

"I *can* do it, just wait. Give me another chance!"

We met him with a chorus of *oh come off it* and waved his words away, telling him not to be stupid. We left it at that but, as you know, Billy didn't.

It did look like he did, at first. He actually did his job like the rest of us for a while. Picking up cigarette butts, bits of plastic, all that which makes its way into the sea when the tide rises and adds a bit more poison to the water. None of us noticed anything out of place, but that doesn't mean that there were no signs. I'm sure there were. I'm sure if we'd paid a little more attention we'd have seen him standing cut out against the sun, watching the waves with sharp, glowing eyes. We'd have seen him look at the stone quayside being built at the far side of the beach.

I was the one who found him. I had stayed behind longer because there was a bus strike and there was no way I'd get home at my usual hour, so I meant to just let myself wander around for a while. I didn't even think to go down to the beach because at that time of night everyone was supposed to be gone. That was why I was so surprised when I started hearing the rumble of machinery, and the cracks and splashes. At first I was stuck in place but then I moved towards the sound, hurrying to the railing over the beach just in time to see Billy of all people in a digger, pushing rocks off the side of the quay and into the water. I shouted his name but there was no way he heard me: he was a man on a mission, his whole focus was on getting those rocks into the water.

But Billy had never even come close to a digger before. He didn't know its controls any better than I do.

Maybe I should have reacted faster, called someone or something. I didn't though. I just ran in bursts towards the quay, calling to Billy. He still didn't hear me. The digger was dusty and phantasmal in the bleak moonlight, and Billy was a whole other person in the automatic yellow light of the machine. It was like watching something on TV, not real life. Sometimes the lines between what's real and what is just pretend blur badly like that, muddle us all up, I think. The point is, there wasn't much I could do, in my state, or in his; Billy was a man possessed.

He didn't even scream as the digger slid backwards, throwing up clouds of fine gravel and dust. The machine struggled for friction but it didn't find any and gravity did the rest, pulling the ghoulish yellow thing into the sea, into the rocks. With it, more debris was dislodged, and a rain of rubble fell over Billy and the digger. There was the sound of glass breaking, metal deforming. The rocks used were heavy and hard. Practically boulders, mountains in themselves.

Billy never stood a chance, honestly.

Still, I leapt over the railing and ran over. There was a lot of stumbling involved, because sand is tricky to run on, always shifting, nothing firm or steady about it, but I think I got there quickly enough. Climbing through the wreckage was harder than it looks on TV, I didn't know where to put my hands or my feet and my weight made some of the rocks shift this way and that, which made the whole process of getting to Billy that much harder. But I did it. I got to him.

He was in bad shape even then. The rocks had broken through the windshield and he was being crushed in a mess of metal and rock and cables. The yellow light had smashed and now flickered in short bursts like gunfire. Billy was bleeding badly, I could see what I think was bone in a couple of places. Definitely nothing I could fix. I saw that right away. Nothing I could do about it. I should have called emergency services, but they'd be on their way, surely, after the fall had shaken the world so much. Everyone in the city must have heard Billy's fall.

I only reasoned that after, to explain how the paramedics eventually arrived on the scene. In the moment I just huffed and puffed, trying to heave rocks off of Billy's body. I kept talking to him – babbling, really, nothing meaningful – and I don't know if it was that or the sudden crunches of pain that woke what little consciousness he had left. He met my eyes after a second and a long groan, which morphed into a wet laugh as his eyes focused on my face.

"How's that," he laughed, merry, his teeth coated with dark spittle. "Think the sea will get the sand now, huh?"

It was so absurd I didn't know what to say. I laughed, and it might have been shock which made me do that. I took Billy's hand, the one missing two fingers, and I squeezed it. I don't know if he felt it. I don't know if he felt much of anything anymore.

"Billy, you crazy fool. Nothing was gonna stop the ocean taking the sand. That's just life. No one can do anything about it, idiot," is what I said. I could hear sirens already. Some part of me thought maybe then this could be okay. If only I kept him awake and talking, maybe he'd be all right.

Billy might have shrugged, or it might have been a cringe, but he was still smiling in that earnest, ridiculous way of his. Nothing about him closed off to the public.

"I did it, didn't I? You guys asked me to."

"We were joking, Billy. Listen—"

"No," Billy cut in. His voice was getting quiet but he was pushing it out of his body with the same zeal that must have made him keep his hands in the water even as his fingers were freezing off. "You needed me to show you it could be done! That's what I did. Is it okay?"

I realised the sirens were too far. They wouldn't get there in time. I still wonder whether Billy heard them or not. He had to know that he was dead, that these were his last instants. That's why he was saying all that stuff, so urgently. That's why I lied to him.

"Yeah," I said. "Yeah, this is what we needed, you're right. Thanks, Billy. It really helped."

Billy laughed again. An exhale of great relief, and there I finally caught a glimpse of how desperate he must have been. Desperate for what? Well, I don't know. I didn't know him well. But maybe he just didn't know how to give any less than this. I said what I said on impulse, you see, because I understood him for a second but I couldn't put my finger on what it was again after, when he'd stopped breathing and the paramedics came and found me there, still holding his hand and talking like a madman. "Thank you," I was saying, I don't know why. "Thank you. It really helped. The sea won't bother your part of the beach anymore, Billy. You did it."

I was given a shock blanket after, while they tried to get his body out of the wreckage. They told me I did everything I could, which is nice of them, I suppose, considering I didn't do much but talk to the kid as he died and hold his three-fingered hand. One paramedic told me it was enough, it was as much as one single person could do for another without putting themselves in danger. I think she's right, and I think maybe that's what Billy didn't get.

I get it now, though. And I can tell when other people understand it. It's not just us beach-cleaners, there are plenty of others who, in one way or another, understand that you can't stop the sea from taking parts of it away even if it kills you. But there's also other Billies out there, and I swear it chills you to see them. Can you imagine what it must be like to live like that? To keep your hands in freezing water as your body screams it's dying just because someone said they need you to do it?

I haven't spoken to Lolo or the lads much since, I mostly just stick to myself. Keep my head down, do the work, you know how it is. I clean Billy's part of the beach too, when I'm not too busy. The quay is almost finished now. I sit there when my buses are late and I watch the sea. My bones creak when I stand up again, dust myself off, and turn my back to the water. I suppose maybe I'm going crazy, but I swear when I'm there, the waves sound just like him, laughing, telling me, *How's that?*

How's that, indeed?

KATHLEEN MACADAM

Kathleen Macadam is a writer from County Wicklow. Until recently she has focused on writing fiction but whilst undertaking the MA in Creative Writing in DCU, Kathleen rediscovered the joy of poetry. She also jumped out of her comfort zone and wrote a screenplay for her dissertation. Her work has been shortlisted and longlisted in several competitions, most recently the Bryan MacMahon Short Story Award 2023 and Write by the Sea Flash Fiction Competition 2023. Her story 'Kilgrey Open Forum' was second place winner in the Allingham Flash Fiction competition 2023. She is working on a novel set in New Zealand, which was longlisted in the Plaza Prizes Crime First Chapters competition 2023. She works in Halfway up the Stairs, a Children's Bookshop in Greystones. Included in this chapbook are three pieces of travel related creative nonfiction.

TWO WEEKS AT SEA - KATHLEEN MACADAM

Aisling and I were sailing up the east coast of Australia headed for the great barrier reef on a yacht called Fuli. We were both in our early twenties. The owner of the boat was a Frenchman in his forties called Jean. The trip from Brisbane to the Whitsunday Islands was due to take two weeks. It felt like two months as the days elongated in front of us. Before leaving Brisbane, we had given Jean money for fuel and food. He didn't buy any food and we ate rice mixed with tomato ketchup, for all our meals. Plus the occasional fish that we caught. One time we had Barramundi.

'Is it cooked?' I asked Jean.

'Yes.'

We devoured it. I enquired further. 'How did you cook it?'

'In lemon juice.'

Aisling and I with our Irish tastes were horrified that we'd just eaten 'raw' fish.

Also on the trip was Manuelle, a friend of Jeans parents who had packed up her life in France to sail around the world with him and an Israeli girl called Limor. After the first week Jean asked Limor to leave, and she was dropped at a marina. I can't remember why Limor was annoying Jean. We learnt the unsettling news during the trip that Jean was looking for a wife. It soon became clear to him that Aisling and I weren't interested. Jean also informed us that he was usually naked when he sailed. We were relieved that Jean fought his natural urges to be nude and wore shorts when we were near him.

When we reached Lady Musgrave Island at the start of the Whitsundays, we anchored the boat and Aisling and I jumped into the clear blue ocean. We felt free as we swam away from the claustrophobia of Jean and the boat. He called us back almost immediately. Cursing him we swam back and climbed up the ladder our faces like question marks.

'There was a shark near you,' Jean casually informed us.

'And you didn't tell us?' I asked incredulously.

'You would have panicked.' He was probably right.

The highlight of the trip was the incredible marine life (with the exception of sharks) such as sea turtles and shoals of tropical fish. Dolphins would frequently swim beside us, playing in the waves at the bow. My favourite time was night watch. Sitting alone under the stars, a path to the moon shimmering on the ocean. I felt at peace.

We were relieved to reach Airlie Beach and say goodbye to Jean and Fuli. Jean deposited Manuelle here as she was irritating him, not to mention impeding his wife search. I felt so sorry for her as she unloaded boxes of books off the boat, her yearlong adventure cut down to two weeks. She looked lost amongst the backpackers.

Fifteen years later, Aisling thought she was hallucinating when she saw a leaflet on the notice board of the Solicitors firm where she works in London. It was a picture of Jean, standing at the bow of Fuli. He was in Bali looking for crew. His search continued.

Lady Elliot Island – The first land in days

SURPRISE BREAD - KATHLEEN MACADAM

In June 1997, a digital clock in Tiananmen Square counted down the hours and minutes until the handover of Hong Kong from the United Kingdom to China. How did I end up seeing this clock in Beijing? After two years backpacking with my friend Aisling in Australia and New Zealand, it was time for us to go home. We had little cash left, no credit cards.

We had a one-way ticket from Christchurch to Hong Kong and onwards from Hong Kong. In Christchurch, the travel agent's nails clicked rapidly on the keyboard as she tried different flight combinations to get us home. There were no flights from Hong Kong to London for months, they were full due to ex pats leaving. The nearest we could get to Dublin was a flight from Hong Kong to Frankfurt, five weeks after we would arrive in Hong Kong. 'We'll take it' I said, and we started planning a five-week budget trip around China.

After the glacial air of the South Island, Hong Kong was hot, crowded, loud. It took a day to get a visa then we boarded a ferry to China. For five weeks we travelled on rickety buses and lived off bananas, bread and the occasional treat of street food, glistening greens and garlic cooked on makeshift open fires. A pocket-sized phrase book was our saviour. We pointed at 'I am a vegetarian' to the delight of vendors who would take the book and flick through it pointing at phrases and smiling. We renamed bread, 'surprise bread' as you never knew what hid inside a plain bread roll, something sweet or a chewy grey meat.

There was a lot of poverty. On an overnight bus to Guilin, we stopped at a remote toilet block, and all passengers were ushered off the bus. The toilets comprised of low walls over concrete gullies and the stench of urine was overpowering.

When we got back on the bus, we saw that our rucksacks had been slashed and our belongings rifled through. We were mildly offended that nothing was stolen, as we owned nothing of value. Whoever was looking in our bags probably felt sorry for us and a little bit disgusted after seeing our dirty, raggedy clothes.

At Guilin, we hired bikes and cycled through remote villages to visit limestone mountains and a bamboo forest. Deeper into countryside, there was straw on the side of the roads and animals wandering freely. At every house people would come out and point at us, sometimes follow us. We always felt safe, our followers were purely curious. It did get tiring though feeling like we were in the spotlight, people pointing and staring wherever we went. After this experience I turned to Aisling and said, 'I never, ever, want to be famous.'

Five weeks later, after the handover of Hong Kong, we flew to Frankfurt. Over two days, we hitchhiked from Frankfurt to Calais. We got lifts mostly from truckers and the route took us from Germany across the bottom of The Netherlands, through Belgium and finally to Calais where we boarded a ferry to Dover. Then we hitchhiked from Dover to Holyhead and finally boarded a ferry to Dun Laoghaire. We were down to our last few coins and had enough change to buy one big mac which we split down the middle. We wished we were eating surprise bread.

The Countdown Clock, Tiananmen Square, June 1997

NO GORILLAS IN THE MIST - KATHLEEN MACADAM

When the plane landed in Nairobi airport in August 1998, I was nervous. Not only because I was travelling on my own, but because it was a week after the American embassy there had been bombed in a terrorist attack.

After a lengthy wait in the hot and crowded baggage hall I realised that my rucksack was not going to arrive. I hopped into a taxi where the driver greeted me with the most beautiful smile. He looked confused.

'Where's your bags?'

'Who knows!' I replied.

He laughed. 'Shit happens!'

My heart pounded when we passed the rubble of the embassy. It seemed unnatural that life was continuing, cars driving, horns beeping, groups gathered on the street selling things. The warmth of the taxi drivers welcome, temporarily distracted me.

A few days later, reunited with my rucksack, I made it to Kampala in Uganda and joined the overland camping tour. We were an eclectic mix of people. The group was comprised of Australians, a few English, one American and me. Allie from Scotland and Lisa from England were our tour leaders, and they took turns driving the truck. Sammy was our Ugandan guide. Part of the trip included camping at Mgahinga National Park where we would trek to see the gorillas in the jungle. The gorillas roam in the forested slopes of the Virunga range of extinct and dormant volcanoes that forms the borders of Uganda, Rwanda, and the Congo.

Two weeks before we arrived in Mgahinga, Rwandan rebels kidnapped four tourists and seven Congolese guides and porters who had been on a similar trek in the region. I couldn't get my head around this, that people like me or my new friends, Suzy, Lisa, or Sammy could disappear in such an unimaginable and horrific way. We were under orders not to leave Ugandan territory. When we were there, the gorillas wandered into areas too dangerous to follow. We had to wait it out until they came back into Uganda. As a result, only half the group got to see the gorillas up close. I didn't get to go but given the recent kidnapping I didn't mind. Suzy took my camera and I treasure the photo she took of a baby gorilla asleep on its mother.

There were many beautiful moments on this three-week trip. Camping beside a Masai village and meeting Masai people, sunset in the Serengeti, a pride of lions snoozing on rocks, zebra and wildebeest in the Ngorongoro crater. Whenever I smell a campfire, I think of this trip, sitting around a crackling fire, a canopy of stars above, the sound of wildlife drifting through the night as we chatted and played cards.

Despite these magical encounters, it was difficult to forget the turmoil and violence in the region and I felt uneasy throughout the trip. On one road alone our truck passed three burnt out buses. As we sat around a smoky campfire one evening, news reached us of the Omagh bombing in County Tyrone. Senseless violence was never actually far from home.

Baby gorilla, Mgahinga National Park Uganda. August
1998

AIDEEN O'REILLY

The absolutely best thing about the MACW to date has been my reintroduction to poetry and, with it, the chance to experience the power of few words over many. To celebrate that, I contribute two sestinas and a haiku.

Before this year I knew what a haiku was. I didn't know what a sestina was or why it needed to exist. All that has changed.

SESTINA 1: YOUNGER - AIDEEN O'REILLY

Early evening from the kitchen calls from my mother
Go call your sisters, as she greets my father,
Home from his day in the world.
Eat together, stay together.
If you don't listen, you'll never learn.
May I get up from the table?

Must we do homework at the table
Quietly? Don't give cheek to your mother.
And she says you're going to have to learn
To listen, with respect, to your father.
Always the hurry, go, go getter
Don't be too early to the world.

When I was smaller, I loved the world.
I would get out there as soon as I was able.
Leave behind the pray together.
Fearless woman or passive mother.
Expecting all of what my father
Seemed to assume was his. Much to learn.

I tried and tried and tried to learn.
I grew more wary of the world.
I doubted more and more my father.
I sulked and slouched at their table.
I railed against the whole thing. Mother,
Honestly, are we in this together?

Paradox and polarity hang together.
It's what I came to learn.
Refusing that paradigm of girl, woman, other.
Long hauling myself across the world
Running to stay stable.
It's the end of the line father.

Private decency no longer cuts it father.
Only public acts can make this better.
Now that we are able and willing to turn that table.
We have by now not much more to learn
Of the ways of that world.
The one that martyred mothers.

Keep turning those tables, there is much yet to learn.
Father, father's father, fathers' sons - all together.
The world was always loaded, as I guess you knew, mother.

SESTINA 2: OLDER - AIDEEN O'REILLY

The woman sits quietly, she is my mother.
She looks through me, I am her daughter.
Remember, from my earliest life.
Remember, we smiled to one another.
Remember chasing about the lawn.
Gentle carer for the crying child.

Yes, it is me, your child.
Yes, smile for me mother.
Remember you sewed me a dress of lawn.
When I was your favourite daughter.
Just that day, over any other.
That day when you were full of life.

How is your life?
Do you know your child?
Could it have been other
Than it has been, mother?
Your saddened daughter
From those days on the lawn.

The blinding green of that lawn,
The certainties of that life
The disappointment in a daughter,
Who stopped being a child
And needed a different kind of mother,
Growing, separating and becoming other.

Faraway, outside your caste, I am other.
I live without certainty or a lawn.
But all of life is good, mother.
There is life beyond your life,
More than one way to raise a child,
More than being a favourite daughter.

I am here, still your daughter.
I will care for you like no other.
I will care for you like my child.
We will sit here on the lawn
Together. While there is life
I will be here with you mother.

A child crawls across the lawn.
A daughter that day like no other.
Full of life, as you still are, my mother.

HAIKU - AIDEEN O'REILLY

Sad by design. Seeks
Answers. Troubled, asks: Tell me
It will be ok?

JANET HAWKINS

Janet loved books from an early age, reading Enid Blyton by the light of the moon when her parents thought she was asleep.

Later in life Janet had the privilege of owning and running a bookshop in the market town of Blessington for over 15 years until Covid closed its doors.

Now studying Creative Writing, Janet is working on her first novel which hopefully will be published in 2024. God willing, touch wood, wind behind her, rub of the green etc…

WHERE MY SOUL LIVES - JANET HAWKINS

Lie in the never-dark of summer and listen to the sea rush on shore, draw breath and rush again.

Atlantic winds will wake you later. Exuberant at finding land after many miles, they will push like rowdy schoolboys, howling around the rafters, rattling windows, snatching things, making them dance just out of reach.

See the ancient turf in modern plastic bags piled across the endless brown, purple, golden, barren bog. A heat wave here is three consecutive days without the need of a fire.

Drive up the mountain roller coaster, eyes on the road, not on the fall. Then down, down to the crystal clear water that turned you blue and made you happy, decades before Lonely Planet told the world about your special beach.

Watch the wind and sun turn the water every shade of grey and green, rose and blue. Rest your eyes where sky meets sea as it always has and always will, long before and long after whatever troubles your heart.

Learn from the mountain. Just be. The clouds wash over Slievemore, always moving on, making room for the sunshine that shines down, glinting from the rock.

I sit and watch the mountain, light and dark giving contrast and definition. Sometimes I am the wind, restless, ever changing, moving to be alive. Sometimes I am the sunshine, intense, bright, fighting the clouds. Here I learn to be the mountain, standing tall, as I am. Grounded in all this beauty the day's weather, the good and the bad, become part of me, without defining me.

Printed in Great Britain
by Amazon

32180151R00066